D0176862

© DANIELLE NAPLES

RACHEL EVE MOULTON

Tinfoil Butterfly

Rachel Eve Moulton earned her BA from Antioch College and her MFA in fiction from Emerson College. Her work has appeared in *Beacon Street Review*, *Bellowing Ark*, *Chicago Quarterly Review*, and *Bryant Literary Review*, among other publications. *Tinfoil Butterfly* is her first novel.

TINFOIL BUTTERFLY

RACHEL EVE MOULTON

MCD X FSG ORIGINALS
FARRAR, STRAUS AND GIROUX NEW YORK

TINFOIL
BUttERFLY

MCD × FSG Originals
Farrar, Straus and Giroux
120 Broadway, New York 10271

Copyright © 2019 by Rachel Eve Moulton
All rights reserved
Printed in the United States of America
First edition, 2019

Grateful acknowledgment is made for permission to reprint the definition of *malignant* from Merriam-Webster.com, copyright © 2019 by Merriam-Webster, Inc.

Library of Congress Cataloging-in-Publication Data
Names: Moulton, Rachel Eve, 1975– author.
Title: Tinfoil butterfly / Rachel Eve Moulton.
Description: First edition. | New York : Farrar, Straus and Giroux, 2019.
Identifiers: LCCN 2018060823 | ISBN 9780374538309 (pbk.)
Subjects: GSAFD: Horror fiction.
Classification: LCC PS3613.O854 T56 2019 | DDC 813/.6—dc23
LC record available at https://lccn.loc.gov/2018060823

Title-page art by Thomas Colligan

Designed by Abby Kagan

Our books may be purchased in bulk for promotional, educational, or business use. Please contact your local bookseller or the Macmillan Corporate and Premium Sales Department at 1-800-221-7945, extension 5442, or by e-mail at MacmillanSpecialMarkets@macmillan.com.

www.fsgoriginals.com • www.fsgbooks.com
Follow us on Twitter, Facebook, and Instagram at @fsgoriginals

1 3 5 7 9 10 8 6 4 2

For Don Wallis

TINFOIL BUTTERFLY

ONE

I swing my body up to the front seat of the van and put my feet on the dashboard. My Doc Martens are filthy, and I wet my forefinger to rub at a particularly offensive patch. It clears a trail that makes the rest of the dust more visible and clods of dirt hit the floor. I roll the window down and release the most offensive chunks into the fresh air.

"Don't worry about it," Lowell says. "It's too fucking cold out there." He pushes his foot down hard on the gas pedal and my sweet Veronica, my name for Lowell's 1980 Vanagon Westfalia, tries to oblige.

"Time is it?" I stretch my arms up in a casual gesture that ends abruptly when my knuckles hit the bare metal ceiling.

"You fell asleep," Lowell says.

"I got that part. Where are we?"

He stretches out his arm to rest on my shoulder, then gives my long, dark hair a little tug that's more affectionate than sexual. I don't like it.

"You look good today, Emma. Better than usual," Lowell says. "I like you. You know that? I really do."

"Sure you do, Lowell, because I'm incredibly likable. Adored by millions. Where are we." It's late October and the South Dakota I fell asleep to was endlessly brown and flat, so boring it put me to sleep. It is nothing like Ray promised. He said the Badlands would be desolate and endless, the kind of unexplored place that you have to stand right up on the edge of before you'll know if you are the kind of person who has the guts to jump.

"Why don't we go back to sleep?" Lowell suggests with a wiggle of his eyebrows.

"Don't be gross. And answer me. Where are we?"

"Where are we? That's what you want to know. We're still in South Dakota. Feels like we've been here our whole damn lives, doesn't it? Piece-of-shit state."

The van smells like the sex we had in it before I fell asleep for God knows how long. I was dreaming of my hair falling out in large chunks of scalp and silky thin threads. Just before I woke up, a man passing by said, "Why don't you knit a blood sweater?" The dream, unlike the gnawing pain in my gut, is unfamiliar.

"Hottest girl I've ever been with," Lowell says, as if

he's making a note to himself to share with his friends. "And that's saying something."

I've hated my body my whole life, but that squirrelly Emma-and-Lowell-humping scent reminds me that breasts, particularly my set of double Ds, are quite useful. That same smell has also convinced me that I hate Lowell. I'm pretty sure he's a serial killer, and if not serial yet, he is certainly on his way to becoming one. He says he's a tattoo artist, studying to be a contortionist, or a contortionist studying to be a tattoo artist, I can never remember which, though the former is the safest bet since he hasn't proven to be particularly flexible. He's headed to "snag" his kid and then on to the West Coast to try out for the Jim Rose Circus. He wants to be there by Halloween so he and his kid can meet Perry Farrell before Jane's Addiction splits. I tell him a twenty-two-year-old-man "snagging" his kid to join a freak show to meet a band makes him a groupie. At best. He shrugs me off. Lowell is the kind of white dude who thinks tribal tattoos are a grand idea. He's plenty tatted up—crucifixes and bleeding hearts seem to be a major theme, but he's got a naked lady on his back with tits nearly as unrealistic as mine and the name of his kid over his heart. I try hard not to find the latter charming.

"You would have fucked me even if I was ugly, Lowell."

"No doubt. Most eighteen-year-old girls are hot. They can't help it."

When I first saw Lowell walking toward Veronica, I was in Lower Michigan, having hitched my first ride on the wrong damn highway. Interstate 70 or Interstate 75. Who could tell the difference really? But then again, I was still dosed up on hospital drugs. It's amazing what they'll give you when they think your pain is physical, mental, inconvenient, and unfixable. Percocet, Vicodin, Lortab. In my bag, I've got a nearly full bottle of Vicodin snuggled in under prescriptions for the other two.

Lowell is my second hitch. Michigan was orange and red with fall when I first met him, although the trees were beginning to thin, hushing the ground with leaves not yet grown brittle. The air was already October crisp. I've been with him thirteen days if you count today. I found him on the outskirts of Detroit, balancing an open beer and a sandwich while trying to dig the keys out of his pocket. He said he was heading to make things right with his ex and their kid. Her family's from South Dakota. By our third day together, Lowell admitted she ran away. "Took my kid and ran home to Mommy and Daddy just 'cause I choked her a little bit."

I saw Veronica and immediately thought: "home." My father loved Volkswagens of all makes and models, and I pegged Veronica for the early '80s variety—before water-cooled engines—as soon as I saw her round, sealed-beam headlights. Unfortunately for me, the first thing I thought when I saw Lowell was "victim." The second thing I thought, as I got close enough to smell the cheap, watery beer, was "Daddy." I know I'm dealing with some sick Freudian shit, but my father was the best kind of alcoholic, jolly and accommodating. Plus, Lowell was hot, my age, and I needed a ride. What else was I to do? I didn't even wait for him to get his door unlocked before I cozied up to him, my eyes wide and helpless, my hands reaching out for a slug of his beer.

Earlier today, I realized I've been wrong. He is not at all like my dad. His ex did not misunderstand him or turn his kid against him. She *fled*. In the Lowell saga, she is the survivor. The one to root for. Lowell, on the other hand, is a man on the verge in the most unsympathetic of ways. An angry drunk. Prone to declarations of love, self-hate, and violence.

This morning, when I woke up with my right hand handcuffed to his left, none of it seemed funny or quirky or implausible anymore. More fucked-up and aggressive than sloppily endearing. The sex I offered got me out of the handcuffs but not out of his van, which is okay, since I've already decided Veronica is *mine*. Fuck Lowell. He doesn't deserve her. I study him now while he drives, not worrying what he thinks of my stare. He is handsome; I have to give him that. Built, probably over six feet. His arms and legs are toned but not bulky. His hair hangs just below his chin when he leaves it down, and he has a scruff on his face that he grooms every morning, spending a half hour each day to make it look like he's spent no time on it at all.

"We both know you love me for my personality," I say.

"Maybe I do," he says. "Maybe I do."

We're driving up, up, up on a road that curls and weaves over unpredictable terrain. There are spots where it's clear the state has tried to blow away the mountain, smooth out the rock and land so the highway can settle in: flat, wide, and undisturbed. It's also clear that at some point the land won the battle and the construction workers went for their last coffee break never to return. They've put so much effort into taming a skinny stretch of road that no one wants to drive on. The places where they succeeded in blasting away at the granite shine wet, wounding the mountain temporarily. The open expanse of rock is moist with its own gradual healing. I imagine the way it will curve out over the road, how it will rumble ever so quietly until thousands of years pass and the road is buried, swallowed up by a swoop of dirt, moss, and tree roots digging deep to hold it all together. I close my eyes to hear the soft whistling push of those roots against the underside of the asphalt.

I've known today was the day since I woke up in the dark with my wrist cuffed to his, and yet it still makes my stomach hurt. My belly, from the button down, is marked up ugly and red, laced like a boot. The pain has been growing behind my scar in spite of the pills, but I've decided to stop taking the Vicodin. To be drug free for the first time in several years. The decision alone makes me feel sweaty, but I want to be sober when I see the Badlands for the first time.

"You can let me out anytime," I say.

"I'm not letting you out in the middle of nowhere."

"It's hardly nowhere. We're here in it, aren't we? It must be somewhere." I never should have taken a nap, but as it turns out, waking up in the middle of the night to realize you've misjudged a situation so terribly that you've gotten yourself properly abducted keeps you awake. This is the day I ditch Lowell.

"Look at you."

I look down at my lap.

"You're still trying to rub the blanket mark off your cheek. It's nearly six p.m., we're in South Dakota, the Black Hills, to be more specific, and it started to snow about five miles back. This is the icy center of nowhere."

"The Black Hills?" I ask. It's farther than I wanted to go. "I want out soon, Lowell. At the next gas station or fruit stand or corn palace or whatever. Ride's over."

He laughs at me like I've just said the stupidest thing in the world.

"Okay, fine. I'll pull over, but first you get in the back."

"What for?"

"You know what for. You owe me."

I should have guessed this was coming. And maybe I did. Maybe I set the whole thing up to play out this way. Maybe I knew he'd turn territorial or even violent and it would make what I planned to do all along seem justified. Maybe.

"Have you ever been to the Badlands, Lowell?" I ask without looking at him.

"Nope. Just drove past it and I gotta tell ya, it didn't look like much."

"How does someone visit South Dakota and not want to go to the Badlands? Let's turn back. You can visit it with me." I'm gathering all my anger for him, putting it in a ball that is filling up where my insides used to be, but I don't need him to know that yet.

"If it were up to me, I'd never have set foot in this state. My ex thought her family would protect her. Dumb bitch. She should have stayed in Michigan with me."

A chill works through me. When I first met him and he was still wooing me, he made it sound like he still loved his ex. Like they would work it out if he could just get to her. A few days ago we stopped at a Kmart and I waited while he picked out T-shirts with rainbow necklines. He bought lace-trimmed socks, a packet of little-girl underwear, and a Snow White toothbrush. I didn't think on it. He called them presents and I accepted that. It wasn't my business. Now I understand that the clothes, this van, the handcuffs, the gun I found hidden in the spare-tire well, are all supplies.

"The Badlands weren't interesting enough to pull you out of that dream you were having about forty-five minutes ago. You were twitching. Pretty funny, actually." Lowell snorts.

He does not deserve this van. He's letting it fall apart. The upholstery on the ceiling is mostly missing, and what isn't hangs down torn and loose around the sides. He's given the outside a new paint job—a baby-poop-brown color—but hasn't bothered to deal with the rust all around the seams. He's covered the front seats with India import blankets because he's lazy. If it were my dad's, if it were mine, I'd fix it up right. My dad could fix any car or bike or truck or van, as long as it was made before 1990. He owned his own garage, and I used to spend days there watching him work. My mom made me go to school more often than not, but when I was sad, Dad'd pull rank and say, "Little Wing, you're working with me at the shop today."

"Map says we're almost to Sturgis. You'll love my kid. I bet you'll be a natural with her," he says, and for the first time, I realize that I am a part of his plan.

"I'm not interested in meeting your kid, Lowell. I need to get to the Badlands." Anger throbs in my voice. He hears it, but he isn't scared. He should be scared.

"For someone who hitched a ride, you sound pretty put out." He puts his hand on my thigh, and his fingers spider crawl their way up toward my hip. "Get in the back."

"Fuck you," I say.

"What's one more good time to you anyway?"

"Lowell, I want out. I haven't got time to mess with you."

"Just get in the back," he says, and swerves. It's a big enough move to make me grab for the door handle.

He's laughing at me. He's glad he can scare me.

"You think I'm gonna crash? I'd never hurt my baby." He pats Veronica on the dashboard. The pat makes me angrier than his hand on my thigh. *This is mine*, I think. *My body. My moment. My Veronica.*

I crawl into the back, stumbling as he makes Veronica hit a bump.

The tiny sink is overflowing with unwashed dishes. I wipe my hand across the Formica countertop. *Poor baby. I'll fix you up.*

The van is still moving along as fast as ever.

I found Lowell's gun a long time ago. He's not a genius at hiding things. But now that I think of it, I didn't find the handcuffs until they were on me. That scares me a little.

I pull back the carpet and ease up the panel that hides the spare wheel. The gun is cold in my hand. I put it in the right pocket of my leather jacket and climb back into the front seat.

All around us the land reaches up toward a starry sky. The world outside is full of thick green pine trees. Remnants of a recent snow sit pristine and white on the boughs high above the ground.

"Pull over, now."

The van does not slow down. Lowell keeps his gaze straight ahead.

"I mean it, Lowell."

Still no response.

"Pull the fuck over, Lowell."

I've been trying to get to the Badlands for months. I've been so close for the past week that I can feel the grit of the land gathering between my teeth.

Ahead the road curves up again. I reach into my pocket, fumble out the gun, almost dropping it, before I hold it to Lowell's cheek.

"You should watch yourself," he says, not even flinching. His eyes stay on the road. "Not everyone is as nice as me."

"You're a fucker, Lowell."

"You going to shoot me? Is that your plan?"

"Yes, that's my plan. I'm going to shoot you and take your van."

"You ever shot anyone before, Emma? It's nasty. Brains and bits and white chunks you won't know what to do with."

"You've never shot anyone. Don't pretend you have," I say, but I'm not confident about this anymore. Not at all.

"You think you can steal my van? What a joke. You're all used up. Don't even have all your parts. That scar on your belly is ugly as hell. No one is gonna want a woman who ain't even got her woman parts."

I take a deep breath. If I'd stayed in the hospital and let the doctor remove the stitches, I might not have such a scar.

I take the gun away from his jaw and swing it at his temple, but I miss and hit above his cheekbone with a thud.

"Owww!" he says, and the van slows.

He is reaching across my body and opening up my door before I understand his intention. Next, he's shoving me, and I'm slipping out into the cold like an idiot.

I float free until the shock of the earth crashes into my hip and shoulder. The ache of it sliding beneath me is sobering. My anklebone hits the grass and gravel at the side of the road and bounces off the frozen earth, sending vibrations up my leg. A fierce pain rips into the palm of my left hand. I hold on tight to the gun, but it clanks out of my fingers as I skid to a halt. I lie still for a second before I can think what to do next. The gun is at least a foot away.

The van screeches to a stop and the door opens with a creak and then slams shut.

A second wave of pain hits me. It hits every part of me, like I've dropped my body into a bucket of ice water and I gasp for air, suck it in, and then hold it tight. All that air and pain burning my lungs. For one strange moment, I think maybe if I stay perfectly still Lowell won't be able to see me, but the sight of his boots only a few feet from me brings me back.

"Get up," he says.

He can't see my face.

"You dead?" he asks with a short laugh.

I don't answer.

"Shit," he says, less confident this time. His boots inch toward my face. I keep waiting for him to pick up the gun. To circle around me and grab it up, but he's still too stupid to know he's in danger.

He gets closer and closer as gravel sifts out from under his feet. I listen and watch, aware of the slow, deliberate movement of his arm through the air as it comes toward my shoulder. The static between his body and mine grows. Just before his fingers brush the naked skin at the back of my neck, I lunge, wrapping my free hand around his wrist and digging my nails in deep. I use his weight to pull myself to my feet. He yelps. I bring my knee to his crotch. He cries out before falling. I step to the right and reach down, scrape fingers through gravel to get the gun in my hand and then I'm off.

There is only an instant of pain before I'm running full speed. Running fast and blind through the trees, gun in my hand, branches lashing at my face, the air too crisp to get a clean breath.

"Come back here!" His voice echoes after me. I keep running, stumbling over scrub, my arms brushing tree trunks. "People die out here!" he shouts, and suddenly he is the good guy.

I stop running once I am far enough into the forest

to be hidden. Veronica's headlights shine in the distance. Her interior light goes on, and I know he is rooting around, looking for something to harm me with.

For one terrifying instant, I let myself feel the insanity of my situation. I'm so fucking sick of myself. My weak side bubbles, percolates brown like coffee. I push it down, hold in the pitiful *why me*? I wrap my fingers in my tangled hair and pull. A hint of red comes away with my fingertips. *Blood Sweater* flashes through my mind as if it's the title of a book of poetry or on a movie poster.

Behind me is darkness. In front of me are Lowell and my Veronica, her headlights still shining into the night. I thread through the trees to come out of the woods in front of the van.

At the edge of the dark, dark wood, I put the gun in my pocket. I step into the middle of the road.

I move right into the beam of the headlights, and Veronica is not fifteen feet away from me. Lowell, back in the driver's seat, turns on the brights. He did not expect me to present myself—a normal girl would stay hidden—and this is part of why he likes me in the first place. I do not flinch. I do not squint. I am not normal. I lower my arms and wait. He could decide to put his foot on the gas, run me over. But he won't. He will see me. He'll think that I need him and this'll make him feel strong, violent. This will be his undoing.

The driver's-side door opens and his boot hits the ground.

"Lowell, please don't leave me here." I sound so sincere.

He says nothing. His boot doesn't move.

"I won't make it out of here alone. I'm scared, Lowell. Please. I made a mistake."

I can't see his face. The headlights are blinding. I want to blink, but I force my eyes to stay open. They begin to water and I encourage them, spilling tears down my cheeks so that Lowell will see I am weak.

"Radio says there's a storm coming," he says. "A big one."

"Help me," I whisper.

"Say you're sorry," he says.

"I'm sorry." I've said it too fast. I should have paused. Struggled a little with the admission. He is quiet for a long time.

"You are not sorry and you are not scared," he says.

I rub my cheeks with the back of my hand.

"I know you, Emma Powers. I know who you are."

I have not told him my last name. In fact, I've told him next to nothing real about me.

"You should read a fucking paper. Turn on the news. Buy a milk carton."

My hand is in my pocket finding the gun.

"I know you, and your brother, Raymond Powers," he

says from behind Veronica's door. "I know they are trying to find you in relation to his death. I could have called you in a hundred times but I didn't. I'm your goddamn hero. You need me."

"I didn't ask you to be my hero."

"You asked for a ride. You let me pay your way." He pauses. "You care about me."

"I don't give a shit about you, Lowell. Step away from the van. I'm taking it."

"I get the impression that you fucked him too. Did you? Your brother? That's some nasty shit."

"He was my stepbrother and it's not your business."

I have this image of Ray that won't leave me. It's this moment somewhere in the mix of the first years of knowing him when we fell asleep in his bed. Both of us kids not yet turned fourteen. I woke up first and there he was next to me. His eyes shut. His lips parted.

"I'm a bad person. I know that. But you're . . . you're fucked up," Lowell says.

"Get away from the van, Lowell."

"No," he says. "They say you're sick. Like you might need care or something."

"You can get the shit you need out of the van and let me go," I say, and bring the gun out of my pocket. I don't point it at him yet, but I hold it at my side away from my body so he can see it. "Turn off the headlights, Lowell."

He moves then. First leaning into the van to turn off the headlights and then putting two boots on the ground.

The absence of the light leaves us in complete darkness. My eyes are slow to adjust, and I can't tell if he has a weapon.

"I'll shoot you in the foot." I take aim at the space below the shape that must be the door.

"You can't possibly hit my foot. You don't know how to shoot."

He's right, but the dark woods are making me feel brave. Veronica is waiting to be saved.

I pull the trigger and am surprised by the kickback and how the noise slices into my brain. I stumble, but Lowell's boots remain firmly on the ground. The bullet has disappeared into the dark.

Lowell slams Veronica's door shut, but the sound of it is low and distant under the ringing of the gunshot still in my ears, my jaw.

"You have to keep your eyes open when you shoot," he says.

"I'll do better next time," I say.

He steps toward me.

"You're shaking," he says. He takes another step in my direction. "I'll make you stop."

His offer is real so I shoot again but see no impact and so I shoot again. This time he sinks. Drops backward and stays there. I've hit him. It makes me giddy. *I did it. I fucking shot you, Lowell.*

I walk up beside him and am proud of myself, my face is flushed, my arms strong.

"Lowell?" I'm standing over him. His eyes are clenched shut, his jaw tight. I look for blood. I expect him to gush—blood and curse words rolling forth—but he is strangely silent, as if he is holding it all in, blood and breath and screams, but then he lets go and the moan is long and bubbly. The blood is pooling around the switchblade he's dropped next to his thigh. I kick the knife away from us and watch it skid under Veronica.

"You fucking shot me."

"Looks like your leg. That's survivable. Do you know how to make a tourniquet?"

"Jesus," he says, but he's awkwardly taking off his belt even as he's saying it. He wraps it around his leg near his groin and pulls it tight.

"You'll have the knife back when I pull away."

I reach for Veronica's door handle.

He leans forward and grabs my ankle, pulls, and I lose my balance. The gun hits the pavement and my head hits the van. I'm on the ground looking up at the starry sky before the world goes black.

When I open my eyes, a dark shape circles overhead. Something come to swoop me up. Lowell's body is under my legs. I've landed half on top of him. Not much time has passed. Minutes? Seconds? We are lying on the asphalt in the dark. Veronica's interior light is the only illumination. Lowell's tourniquet is now in place and there is blood on my clothes. I roll off of him.

My head aches but I focus on standing and gaining distance from Lowell.

"You'll die out here," he says. "Snow's coming. A blizzard. I can smell it. You don't have any idea what you're up against."

I open the back of the van and pull out some blankets for Lowell. Some energy bars. A bottle of water. My head is thudding.

"You shot me," he says when I return. He's breathing hard now. The pain is getting to him. "Good for you. I didn't think you could."

"I could and I did. I'll get to a gas station and call 911. They'll be out here in a few hours. Maybe we'll both live through the night."

"I'll tell them who you are and where you're going."

"You do that," I say. The Badlands are close, and what Lowell doesn't understand is that once I'm there I've reached my goal. What happens after that doesn't matter.

"You don't know anything about these hills," he says. And he's both right and wrong. Ray taught me a lot about them. I know, for example, that they are a small and isolated mountain range with such extensive tree coverage that they look black from a distance. The Lakota Sioux believed that if seen from above, these hills would look exactly like the human heart.

"I'll find a pay phone as soon as I can," I say.

The gun is where I dropped it so I grab it and shove it back in my pocket. I hop inside the van and pull the door shut.

"Emma!" Lowell begins to scream, and it is genuine this time. Terrified. "At least leave me some drugs."

I crack the window enough to say, "I'll send help."

"You can't let me die out here. I have a daughter."

"You'll be fine," I say, and start the engine. It's the exact line Ray and I used to say to each other when life got to be too much. The last time I said it was just before I let him die.

TWO

I sing along with "Jane Says" by Jane's Addiction as loud as I can. I beat my hurt hand against Veronica's steering wheel as Lowell's mixtape gives me voice. With the windows rolled up and the dark pressing in, Farrell's words keep me driving.

This Black Hills highway, with the dense woods on my right and a bottomless drop-off on my left, is too narrow to turn around on so I keep going up, up, up into the increasing darkness of night before I start making turns onto side roads that I hope will lead me back down.

Harney Peak is the highest point in these black mountains, but if this is 244 like I think it is, Mount Rushmore can't be more than a dozen miles away. Civilization of some kind should feel closer. There is surely going to be a tourist stop or public restroom. So far, nothing.

Veronica is about out of gas. I couldn't go back for Lowell even if I wanted to and I don't want to. There is a fork in the road ahead, a patch of clear black breaking up the otherwise perfect line of trees, and Veronica inches forward toward the dark, turning right just as the moon slides behind a cloud. I flip on her brights. The road snakes through pine trees for a few miles before it becomes more pothole than road.

Something's up ahead. A building? It shines in the dark despite the lack of moonlight. The road straightens out and Veronica eases into a large parking lot before she sputters to a halt and dies.

"I'm sorry, sweet girl." I rub the dashboard with the palm of my bloodied hand. The pain zips up my arm, grounding me.

The place is deserted. On the other side of the empty lot, there are two gas pumps, a phone booth, and an old silver dining car. Ray told me about the ghost towns in these Black Hills. Abandoned buildings from the gold rush that still stand, stubborn. He'd hand me facts about a time or place, something dark he was obsessing over, and I'd weave it into a story in which we were the heroes. Ray loved my stories. In them we were powerful, facing the decaying buildings and bodies with equal parts ferocity and humor. This diner looks just like the kind of place he would have given me, putting his head in my lap so I could run my fingers through his hair. Back when I calmed him. When I helped him shut his mind down so he could dream of things not quite so dark.

The moon pushes out from behind a cloud, bright and full, and the diner shines its full silver. Below a row of windows that stretch across the front are the words "Good Food" and above the windows in larger block lettering EARLENE'S DINER.

I put Veronica in neutral. The wind whispers high up in the trees. The only sound. Once out in the cold, I put my weight into her doorframe to push her across the lot. A light snow begins to fall. Veronica rolls grumpily forward.

"There could be gas in those tanks, old girl. I know you're hungry." I push Veronica as close to the gas pumps as I can and then jump back into the driver's seat, pushing down the parking brake with my left foot just before she hits the old-fashioned pumps.

My eyes adjust a bit and the moon obliges by peeking down at me so I can lift one of the gas pumps and apply pressure. No gas comes out, not a drip.

"It might not mean there isn't any," I say to Veronica. "It could just mean I need some sleep and sunshine to figure it out."

The woods are quiet. I let myself notice that now. The forest gives off an unnatural, deafening silence. Ray would say, "This land was promised in perpetuity to the Lakota Sioux in 1868 and then we took it back as soon as we found gold. That's the silence you hear, Emma My Emma. A silence we white people bloodied ourselves for." Ray always spoke like that, with the full drama of having been there. Culpable in ways that he could not imagine his way through. And that was his problem, really. In his art and in his mind. Ray would find a horror to circle and he'd feel it with his whole person, researching it until there was nothing left to read and then regurgitating the information in various art forms—painting the same bloody black hole of history over and over again until the obsession became so self-indulgent, so personal and painful that he'd break from the world for a while, shutting himself in his room for days.

Ray was a welder, a painter, a muralist. His best work came from his darkest moments and so I never stopped him when he was in the midst of it. Never said enough is enough. Not until he was exhausted and weepy from lack of sleep. Then, and only then, I'd soothe him. Interrupt the circle of thoughts he was trapped in and talk to him until he slept. I see now that another person, a less selfish person, would have tried to stop him long before he needed me, but I always wanted to see what he'd make next, and if I'd be in it. I longed to be that horror, the thing he obsessed over for so long that he understood and loved all of its truths and ugly spots and yet still wanted to know more. I wanted to be his muse.

A breeze picks up, the light snow floats across the lot toward the diner and the tiny scattering sound, as quiet as it is, breaks the spell. The diner door is ajar, I see that now, and the wind is moving toward it, as if the building is breathing in. Its inhale pulls at my body, tugs at the hairs on my arms.

Then there's a scraping noise that is not the wind.

"Hello?" I say.

It's coming from the side of the building. There is a five-foot gap between the diner and the phone booth and from inside that dark hole someone or something is watching me. The sound comes again, like something is being dragged along the diner's metal frame.

As the moon makes a full appearance, I move to the outside curve of the diner car. I see it. A glare, a shine of silver that isn't the diner. A pair of eyes, human eyes. Green and bright and peeking out from behind the eyeholes of a mask that looks winged.

The creature stares back at me for one held breath before it turns to run.

I leap forward, five long strides to the edge of the building but I'm standing alone. There's nothing. No one.

I'm tired. I have to pee. I need sleep. I need perspective. Surely some sunshine will make everything seem doable.

There is a smear of blood on my jeans so wide and thick that I know there is no getting rid of it. It's Lowell's. Better-off-dead roadkill Lowell. I move to the phone booth and once inside, see that I am shaking. My hands make the receiver clatter against the metal before I yank it back. I dig into my inside pocket where I keep my medication. A nearly full bottle rattles comfortingly. I take one. Just one pill and the peace of it settles in my throat, my belly, my veins. One pill doesn't mean I haven't quit.

Lowell is probably already dead.

There is a dial tone. My heart leaps and I push 911. The numbers beep back at me but then the dial tone returns as if unaware of my request. I try it again. Nothing. This is when I look up and notice the sign in the booth. I pull my Zippo out of my pocket and hold it up high. A big ape of a man with fangs dripping blood, hair all over his face, his arms too long for his body. The words above him big and bold as if announcing a movie premiere: BIGFOOT SIGHTING? REPORT YOUR FINDINGS. DIAL 555.

Like a fool I dial 555.

"Hi and welcome to Earlene's Diner where the incredible can happen. From finding the best pancakes in South Dakota to finding your own nugget of gold. Think you've seen the Sasquatch? Leave us your story and make a wish."

The voice is followed by a beep and then silence.

"The Sasquatch lives in the Pacific Northwest. I'm not in the fucking Pacific Northwest." I slam down the phone. My hand rests on the receiver and the moon slides out, shines through the glass of the booth like the sun, and there is blood under my fingernails. It looks like dirt.

I rub it on my jeans, but the blood is there too. Most of it is Lowell's and there is no getting rid of it. No calling for help. No finding Lowell again. The pain in my belly shoots through me harsh and fast, and I crouch down into a ball in the booth. The pill isn't quick enough. Not one anyway. Two would be perfect, but I'm going to hold back. Wean myself.

Ray had an intimate knowledge of genocide and atrocity and the Lakota Sioux were a particular fascination. He built himself up a hatred for humanity so thick it could not be undone.

I push back the pain to rise and dial 555. When prompted, I say, "I shot a man. He's in the hills. Bleeding out on the side of the highway. Someone should find him before he is all the way dead."

I stick my hands in my armpits to steady them and exit the phone booth. The snow is falling, fast enough to make me keep my chin down. I put all of my weight into the door of the diner to get it to budge. It shudders with effort, and then stops after ten or twelve inches, stuck solid on the warped tile floor. I slip in.

Once fully inside, I raise my lighter again and flick it back on. The flame doesn't do a whole lot, but I hold it up anyway for the little bit of light that it does give. It's a small diner with only a few booths against the front wall and a long counter with a dozen or so stools. I can make out salt and pepper shakers, the coffee station, and strange little figurines lining the high shelf behind the counter. The place is remarkably tidy. The napkin dispensers are full and everything sits in its place.

The air is warm, much warmer, in fact, than an abandoned building has any right to be. I reach into my jacket pocket. The pill is tiny in my hand. What harm can it do? I swallow and the pain turns to a soft, warm fuzz—a ball of fur I can manage, cradle, tickle behind the ears.

I shouldn't be *here*. I realize it fully and confidently even as my sweetly dulled senses keep me still. There is a threat here that I can't see or name. Something that wants me.

My father used to tell me evil had to be invited in. "It's like a friendship at first," he said. "You have to want to be friends with it. Open the door wide and let it play with your toys." He used to rattle my Tonka trucks in my face with a goofy smile meant to look menacing and say, "The devil made me do it." We had a routine, a little one-act play, that we'd do standing across the room from each other, me fidgeting and hopping—giggle-girl anxious:

"Daddy, are you the devil?"

"Hell yeah, pumpkin."

"Will you play with me?"

Then he'd run to me and lift me up above his head to spin me Supergirl style.

My dad's point, I think, was that evil doesn't take people by surprise. In order for it to really get you, a tiny piece of you has to want it. He sure wanted it, my father. He drank it up until he lay down on the train tracks where he let it kill him. Literally let it split him in half. And that's what I tried to do too, right? It's what I'm still trying to do. Split myself in half.

In the warm, moonlit gloom of the diner, I search the wall and find light switches. I flip them all on and turn to face the long room. Their low hum kicks in. I see signs everywhere that once stated the obvious: COFFEE. CIGARETTES. PIE. THIS HERE IS SOUTH DAKOTA. Proud pictures of anonymous Native Americans on horseback. A wooden carving of just a head. Pictures of horses and buffalo. The inside of the diner has been cleaned recently. The shiny curl of the stools, the edge of the countertop, and the shelves along the back wall. It all sparkles.

The counter splits at the midpoint. Behind it is a swinging door with a diamond window of glass that must lead to the kitchen. I've triggered the lights in the kitchen too and they shine proudly through the diamond window.

I'll check the kitchen for food. Then head back out to Veronica for the night.

Through the swinging door there is a small kitchen fully stocked with pots and pans. The grill with an oven below sits in front of me and to my right is the silver door of a walk-in freezer. To my left is a prep station.

"Diners are for waking you up and bars are for putting you back to sleep," I say aloud in homage to my father. He would have wanted to bring this place back to life. Ray would have wanted to burn it down.

I still the swinging door behind me. With it closed, the kitchen feels safe. Almost cozy. The refrigerator is empty, the air inside of it warm, but when I open the metal cupboards, I find neatly stacked cans of beans and corn. Tomato sauce. Tuna. The cans are ordered, arranged with the labels out. I pull out a can of black beans, find a can opener, and a small pot. The stovetop clicks once, twice, and then the flame leaps up. At least one tank is still full on this property. I find some old spices and a spoon. I turn on the oven and open the door so the heat of it fills the room. With my back to the freezer, I eat the beans from the pan.

The warmth of the oven loosens my muscles further. I feel floppy. Soft. I'll rest for a minute. My eyes burn when I shut them. I'm drifting, drifting, gone.

I wake with my hands on my forehead. The stove is still on. I can feel its heat, and I sit up and pull my boots away. The rubber soles are warm. The eyelets burn too hot to touch. My throat is sore. How long did I sleep?

The narrow kitchen spins, and I press my hand to my stomach. I have to pee or puke or both. I turn off the stove and test the kitchen sink to see if there is running water but the pipes don't even groan; they've given up long ago. When I feel steady, I push out into the dining area. The building is empty. Outside, morning has arrived.

The sky is yellow and pink, and the world isn't so scary. I walk across the parking lot—avoiding the spot where I saw that masked creature last night and find a space to squat and pee. The ground is brown with pine needles and shiny with frost. My urine is hot. A faint steam rises.

The world is steadier, warmer once I've finished peeing.

All my aches and pains holler, but yesterday's damage isn't too bad. The air is crisp, and the pavement is slick enough to skate across.

The diner remains warm compared to the outside world. I'm hungry, and I pull another can of beans down off the shelf. I put it all in a pot to heat, but the burner won't light this time. There's just the noise of the gas clicking on so I reach for my lighter. But it isn't in the pocket where I always keep it. It isn't in any pocket. I see it on the counter next to the stove and snatch it up. I know I didn't put it there. I'd never leave it out like that. *Pills.* It's my next thought and shame comes with it. I search my pockets. They are gone.

A low thump. And then another from beyond the kitchen door. It's a purposeful sound.

A fist against a door, perhaps. A rap against a countertop, probably.

"Is someone there?"

I push open the kitchen doorway and stand still. The room appears to be empty. The silence and the growing daylight make me feel confident even as my heart begins to pound faster.

The door swings shut behind me; it flaps freely back and forth.

"Do you know how to get to the Badlands? I'm lost, actually." I touch the rough edge of the counter with my fingertips. "I'm stepping out from behind the counter now," I say. My blood is beating heart-attack fast.

There's a click, a familiar noise. It's Lowell's gun, held by a little boy and pointed at me.

He's young. Maybe seven or eight. A silver mask obscures his face. It looks as if it's made of tinfoil, crumpled and shaped into wings. His eyes, nose, and lips peek through. The mask is beautiful. His fingers on the gun are dirty.

"Hello." A greeting that comes out too loudly against the silence and then I hear the shot. It's deafening. The room comes alive as my heartbeat increases, pumping through my limbs, climbing up into my ears and mouth. I smell the gas burner still trying to light and the little boy's sweat. He exhales in a way that makes me worry he's been holding it in since I first arrived at the diner. The gun drops to the floor.

My eyes stay with the boy as he pushes through the door and out into the light.

THREE

There is a neat little hole in the tin roof behind me.

Lowell's gun rests on the black-and-white tile floor. The kid has dropped it near the door in his rush to get out. I move forward and pick it up. The barrel burns the skin at the small of my back as I stick it in my pants. I let it burn even as my jacket catches on the doorframe and I step out into the wintry world. The kid is standing perfectly still, watching me from around the corner of the diner. The shiny curves of his mask camouflaged by the shiny curve of the diner.

The mask covers up his features, all except his too-green eyes. Fierce as a cat's.

"Why did you try to shoot me? I ought to kick your tiny ass," I say to get some sense of authority back. He's shaking. He's wearing dirty jeans and a flannel shirt over a fisherman's sweater. His tiny fists are clenched so tightly that I worry he's going to make himself bleed.

"Shit, kid . . ." I pause, unable to think what I should say next. "I just needed to get warm. I'll head out as soon as I can. I'm trying to get to the Badlands."

"I've seen you before," he says.

"I don't doubt that. Last night, right? That was you?"

The air is crisp with cold but with the sun out it feels good. He's still shaking.

"Are you cold?" I ask.

"Nobody comes up here anymore."

"I see that. Are you from here?"

"This is where I live," he says.

"Were you born here?"

"Nobody gets born here. Not anymore."

"I'm from the Midwest." A new tactic.

"I only remember here."

"Should we introduce ourselves properly? Shake hands?" I step toward him but he jerks back.

"You have blood on you," he says. I look down at myself and see the smear of it in the sunlight. A rusty brown extends from my right hip to my left thigh. The fingernails of my right hand are encrusted with it.

"I had an accident." I hold out the hand I scraped in the fall from Veronica as if showing him my rug burn of an injury is enough of a confession to put him at ease.

"I like your camper," he says.

"Isn't it awesome? It's a Type 2 T3 with an air-cooled engine," I say. "They started making 'em with water-cooled engines after that. Both have their problems but this is a good one. I know how to keep it running." The little boy is staring at me. I've nerded out on him a bit. "I mean the roof lifts up and it's got a tiny stove and fridge and everything."

"Cool," he says. "Where did you get it?"

"I'm sorry?" I ask, and then add, "I got it at the car place. Where people get cars. What kind of question is that?" I feel myself redden.

"Just never seen one like that."

"Oh yeah? Well, my father owned his own shop so . . ."

"Can I see inside?" he asks.

"Don't you think we should introduce ourselves before I let you see inside my van?"

He keeps his eyes on my face and his hands on the side of the diner. I take one step toward him. Then two. Hand extended to shake hello. Three. As I'm about to reach him, wrap his small fist in my open hand, he bolts, disappearing into the woods.

"Hey!" I yell after him. "I just need gas!"

Alone again. The woods are silent. Dead.

His question *Where did you get it?* echoes in my head. I have a sudden image of Lowell crawling toward me, creeping up behind me to pull me down into the ground, but when I spin around, there is only Veronica and the empty lot, pine trees, and more pine trees.

"Good morning," I say to Veronica. I walk to her and rest my forehead on the passenger-side window. She is icy with frost, but I keep my head to her glass and let the cold burn my skin. "I'll get you out of here. Don't worry."

The snow is holding back for the time being, but the sky has an overall gray look that suggests the snow won't wait much longer. I can see the start of the potholed road from where I sit. It's the only way out. There has to be some reasoning behind the location of the diner, obviously faulty reasoning, considering the current state of things, but someone must have thought it was a good idea at one point. If I can get even a little gas out of the pumps, this place will prove a great discovery.

I put my hands in my jacket pockets and find one of Lowell's cigars remains. I hid the whole lot of them from him back when I got sick of smelling them.

Lowell showed me how to smoke one. He explained there is an art and leisure to it, but I can't get over the smell or how fat it is compared to a cigarette, so undeniably a phallus.

"Can I try?" The boy's voice startles me.

I turn slowly. There he is. Ten steps away, looking at me. He is so young. A little boy with a stray-dog look, and I have the urge to move the layers of clothing from his neck to check for tags.

"Don't you think it's kind of rude to shoot at people?"

It's funny but even looking at him full-on, I can't tell any more about him than I could with a ten-second glimpse. His dirty blue jeans are so long that they drag underneath the heels of his Christopher Robin boots. The mask is intricate, bigger than I'd thought, wings stretching above his forehead.

"Can I have a cigar?" The repeat question allows me to watch his face as he talks. The mask isn't fluid; it's stiff and doesn't move from its spot even to make room for his words.

"How old are you?"

"Twenty," he says. He takes a step forward with his hand held out for the cigar.

"You are not twenty."

"Okay, I'm twelve."

"Liar."

He drops his hand to his side, and I realize I'm not ready for him to disappear. I hold out the cigar as an offering of sorts to keep him with me. He takes it quickly, snatching it in a movement that reminds me of a squirrel, and then steps backward, never taking his eyes off me. He plops down cross-legged on the pavement and sticks the cigar in the back pocket of his jeans.

"You'll crush it," I say and sit down again.

"I don't smoke. That's bad for you. So are those pills."

"Then give them back to me," I say, hoping he can't see my heart beat faster under my layers of jacket and shirt.

"I can't give them back. Those are gone, and I'll make art with the cigar."

"Art? Out of a cigar?" I ask.

"I preprapose things. My mom taught me."

"Preprapose? You mean repurpose?"

"Yeah, repropose."

"Is your mom here?" I ask.

"She's not alive here anymore."

"I'm not sure what that means but I'm sorry to hear it," I say. "Nice mask. What are you supposed to be?"

"I'm supposed to be a boy."

"That part is obvious."

"Thank you," he says. "Actually, it's a special butterfly mask to attract the birds. I made it out of things I found," he says.

"Do birds eat butterflies?"

"Sure. They are garbage eaters. Insects, carcasses, trash but mostly they like the shine of it. They like the diner too. I keep it all shiny for them."

"Do they like guns?"

He thinks about this one, touches what would be his cheek if he weren't wearing the mask.

"I'd never shoot one if that's what you mean."

"You're not a killer then?"

"I didn't say that. Not really. Lotsa things to kill around here but I wouldn't shoot one of the birds. They carry history in 'em. I call them hill gobblers. If you cut one of 'em open, neck to a-hole, you'd find stories in there. So many stories."

"That's gruesome," I say. "I used to call Ray, my stepbrother, Gobs."

"I'm gruesome," he says, clearly pleased. "And why Gobs?"

"Nothing. No reason, I mean. So, really, why the mask?"

"Really?" he asks, and tilts his head at me, birdlike. He's all neck and long gangly legs. His pink lips chewed raw with worry.

"Sure, why not?"

"Burnt. Whole side of my face is gone." He nods his whole head, mask and all, as if to say, *Yep, yes, ma'am. Looks like ground meat all up in there.*

"You're lying."

"I'm not. Pinkie swear," he says, and holds out his pinkie to hook mine. I ignore it.

"You are not burnt, and you are not twelve."

"I'm five."

"You aren't five!"

"Okay, I'm eight, and I'm all burnt up."

"Eight I'll believe."

His pinkie is still held out between us and so I reach out and wrap it with mine. His hands are rough and chapped. He gives me a hard shake and then lets go.

"How did it happen? The burn, I mean."

"Ligh'ning bolt. Slid right down and whacked me in the face."

"Lightning? Come on," I say.

"My daddy can control the weather. He can make it snow or rain or hail or lightning bolt my face. He wanted a girl. He got me, so BAM he lit me all up."

"Jesus," I say before I even give myself a second to think too long about what his daddy might have done to him, lightning or no lightning.

"No, not Jesus. My daddy. And you're gonna need a hat. It's gonna snow. Do you have a hat?"

"You're fucking with me, right?"

"No, a hat is essential. And mittens," he says. He's earnest. Thoughtful even. "George wants that gun," he says with his eyes steady on mine. It's a non sequitur, and not at all a request.

"Who is George? And who's Earlene by the way? And he can't have my gun. That's crazy."

"Can I have it?"

I laugh loudly as an answer.

"You gave me a cigar."

"A cigar and a gun are two very different things. And I need my medicine back."

"I needed it for him."

"Are you George?"

"Nope," he says, and stands up. "I'm Earl," he says. "Can I have it or not?"

"Nope," I say, imitating his inflection, and just like that, before the word is even able to float down and splatter around our feet, he's gone.

"Hey!" I try to stand up as quickly as he has but my head spins. My knees feel weak, and I have to steady myself on the building. By the time I'm ready to run after him, he's gone.

It's time to get moving, to feed Veronica, and get to the Badlands. I stretch. Arms to sky and then down to pavement. I need gasoline. I'm sweating a little. How many hours until withdrawal symptoms appear?

"Hey, kid!" I cup my hands around my mouth and shout out into the incline of pine trees.

"What?" His voice comes from over my shoulder and I jump, hand to heart.

"Christ, kid. How do you do that?"

"Do what?"

"Appear like that. Like you're some kind of fucking ghost."

"I'm not a kid. I'm almost twelve and you shouldn't curse."

"You are not almost twelve. Eight, I believe, and eight is not almost twelve. It's almost nine, depending on when your birthday is. And really, there's no need to sneak up on me. I have the creeps already."

"George wants that gun."

"Well, Emma wants that gas. Do you know how to use these gas pumps?"

"No," he says. "I'm a kid."

"Okay, well, when's the last time someone used them? Are they dry?"

"No one comes here. Not ever."

"Great. Do you have family nearby, or a car? And, if you're Earl, is Earlene your mother? I just need a little bit of gas and then I'll get out of your hair."

"Just me, George, and some version of Mama. Been that way for a while."

"Okay, well, I need gas so I suppose that means I need to meet George."

"You won't like him."

"I expect I won't."

"We can go meet 'im now if you want. You wanna?"

"I don't know. You tell me."

"He used to know how to get gas out of the pumps. Also, I gave him your pills."

"I don't need 'em," I say but even saying it makes me feel shaky.

"You said they were medicine."

"I said I don't need them anymore. Lead the way," I say. This answer puts a swagger in Earl's step, and it occurs to me that he's putting me through some kind of test. There was a right and a wrong answer to this last question of whether or not I wanted to meet the infamous George. I'm not sure if I've passed or failed.

FOUR

Daddy longlegs are the best," Earl says. "They live the longest. 'Cause their legs are so long and thin. I've picked all eight legs off the same daddy longlegs and it still went on living. It couldn't move, but it was living."

Earl is leading me up the steep slope of woods behind the diner. I'm out of breath while Earl barely seems to notice the steady incline of the land. It occurs to me that we are at altitude and my body isn't used to it. The Black Hills get to just over seven thousand feet at their peak and I'm a sea-level kind of girl. We are following a narrow, well-worn path on the forest floor, only as wide as one of his red-rain-booted feet. I glance up from my climb to watch how he uses his hands when the hill gets too steep, maneuvering on all fours when it suits him. His hands are almost as red as his boots, chapped and raw, nails bitten to the quick. His butterfly mask sticks out shiny on either side of his head and is tied with a simple silver ribbon that disappears into the back of his matted dirty-blond hair.

"You're into bugs then?" I ask.

Ray once showed me how to get a bumblebee to land on my finger so I could pet it with my pinkie, reach up right behind the wings and stroke down. The bee would stay still for me. Antennae and legs thread-skinny, body purring.

"It's not just bugs. I love all creatures," he says, and reaches around the back of his head to tighten the bow of his mask. "Big ones and small ones. I like seeing what makes a thing work," he says. "Did you know that monarch cat-a-pillars shed their skin four times before they become a butterfly? Also, night butterflies have their ears on their wings so they can hear the crows and the bats coming for 'em at dusk." Earl stops short, turns to face me, and holds out his arms from his sides to show me his wingspan.

"The crows out here are huge," I say.

"They mate for life, bet you didn't know that, and they're songbirds. All crows are," he says, proud of himself.

"I did not know that."

"I'm very scientific," he says. "I like experiments.

Every time I meet a new person, I try to decide how long they'll live if I pick them apart." Earl stops on the hill and turns to face me. His voice is low and serious. If he weren't so slight, barely reaching my chest and far too skinny, I would be scared. "It's fun to figure out which parts to take off first," Earl continues. "A leg. An arm. With some people, I make sure to take their head off right away so they won't scream. I'd take your head off last."

Earl turns. Starts up the hill again. The terrain is getting steeper. I shorten my stride and find my balance with my hands on a tree trunk.

These hills are full up with green pines and the air carries their syrupy scent—if not for the early cold this year thinning everything out, that smell would stick to the skin it's so thick. The ground is littered with the browned needles of the trees and large rocks jut up bald and lonely and thick as houses. I did not expect the rich desert red that stripes some of these otherwise gray rocks.

Under our feet there are caverns. I know this from Ray. Some are natural but most are abandoned mines. Settlers blasted deep into this rock to root out what they collectively decided was the most precious thing, ignoring the fact that, once dug out, it becomes an excavated organ, robbed of life. The steady rock and the reaching trees do not reveal the fragility of this wormholed place.

"Why wouldn't you take my head off first?"

"You'd have something to say when it came to the

very end." Earl stops again to answer me, and I have to rock back to avoid running into him. My hand reaches out, and I see the blood on my skin as Earl sees it. Some of it mine, my palm raw, but the rest of it, up under my nails and smeared across the back of my hand, someone else's.

"I could kill you. No one would know," he whispers. Earl and I are face-to-face.

"Keep walking and try to remember I'm the one with the gun." I make a shooing gesture.

He turns without hesitation and reinitiates the hike.

"My mom says this is the loneliest place in the whole world."

"She obviously hasn't lived in Southern Ohio."

"Close though, actually," he says excitedly. "She grew up on the Ohio River. In Switzerland County. Isn't that a funny name for a place in Indiana?"

"It is."

"Her daddy was an artist like me. It skipped her and flew straight to me."

"Did he live here with you too?"

"Opa? No. He died. That's how George bought this place."

"I'm sorry to hear that," I say. "The dying part anyway."

Earl shrugs.

We walk in silence. Minutes pass.

Something shines in one of the nearby branches. A small tinfoil bird hung on nearly invisible string. Earl looks at it and then at me, checking to make sure I've noticed, but then there are more, unmissable hundreds. Different kinds of birds and flowers but also elephants and jungle cats and buffalo. Some hang in groups, mobiles made of twine and sticks and husks of flowers. I reach out and let a tiny horse rest in the clean skin of my unhurt hand. It slides from my palm as my body moves forward. It glides back and forth in the cold South Dakota air.

Earl is watching me.

There are carvings peeking out of the pine needles and tired growth on either side of the trail: salamanders; a long driftwood-colored snake whose curvy body shows off the knots of a time when it was simply a tree branch; three baby mice, one overturned; a spider's web that he's used to connect two tall trees, the spider shining out from the middle of the web. My eyes feel hot and I reach up to rub them to find the start of tears.

Ahead Earl pauses to adjust an object. He steps off the path, looking over his shoulder at me. His boots all but disappear into the browning undergrowth. As he leans over, I see each of his vertebrae through his layers of flannel and sweater.

Ray stopped eating at the end of his life. He wanted to feel the life go out of him, and I didn't tell him I thought that was bullshit. I let him do it. I watched. He buried his body in clothes so no one would notice, and I ate his food for him. Put on ten pounds, fifteen, twenty.

I stopped touching him then too. The intimacy that we'd so long shared was gone. I couldn't stand the sharpness of him or how his veins bulged out, pinchable. His skin so thin that if you even bumped against him a great blue blossom would bloom in that spot.

"Who takes care of you, Earl?" I ask even though I know the answer is no one, and in asking, my hand twitches at my side, as if my body wants to reach out to Earl. I shove my hands in my jean pockets.

"I'm not a baby."

"This George dude. He's your father?"

"He says he is."

"He must be proud of all your art."

"'If you can't sell it, it ain't worth nothin','" Earl says in a gruff voice.

"How long have you lived here?" I ask, changing tack.

"We've been here two Christmases. Next week will be our second Halloween. George moved us out here, then he ate up my mother."

"He did not eat up your mother."

"Course he did. He bought her a ghost town, made us move here, and then he ate her."

"I've never heard of anyone buying an entire town."

"I speak only truth."

"Only liars say they never lie."

"My mom says we're all liars. Liars and ghosts."

"You mean said."

"Sure, said. She says we carry with us all the things we've acclimated."

"Accumulated?"

"Like you've got that scar on your belly . . ."

"When did you see my scar?" I instinctively pull my shirt down, as if there is some hope of covering a sighting that already occurred.

"When I took your gun. Your shirt was all bunched up," Earl says, but he does not break stride. "Something happened to you and so you got scarred. Ghosts are like that too. Like scars. They travel with you."

"So where's George? That's what I'd like to talk about. We've been walking a long time."

"Black Hills are made up of 1.25 million acres."

"Are we walking all of 'em?"

"George bought 6.1 for $249,000 back in 1990. Read about it in a magazine and moved us out here straightaway. When he's dead, it'll be mine. One hundred percent of it.

"The town is supercool. It's got an old church, a post office, a grocery. Big old house for living in. It just wasn't near as livable as George thought and you can't never get to it from a main road, especially not in the winter, so Mom opened that diner down there far from the town but nearer the road. That way we could tell diner customers about the mysterious town through the woods. George was gonna build a gravel road from one to the other. Turned out even the diner is too hard to get to most of the year. They don't plow out here. Spring is just as bad. Mom said we should make a commune out of it but George hates people so I figure we just have to get rid of George, then Mama will be back and we can love this place proper like."

"When did you last see her, your mother?"

"Those days add up to too many."

"That I understand," I say, anxious for the days back to Ray to be too many to track.

"Here we are," Earl says.

And then there it is just ahead of us, a wide plateau of land dotted with brown boulders that look like they've been dropped from the sky. Spruce trees sit on the edges of the plateau. On the far side, facing us, is a row of buildings that lean softly to the right as if they are putting all their exhausted weight into their one good hip.

Like the diner the buildings are aptly labeled: SALOON, POST OFFICE, GROCERY, CHURCH. They are painted garish yellows and ketchupy reds, although any paint job was clearly done some time ago. The beaten-down wood shows through, raw and indignant. The remnants of a truck, hood open, guts gone, sit sadly in the tall grass. A smattering of tree stumps in varying states of decay sit in the barren field between where we stand and the storefronts. A rusted chain saw tilts sadly against a skinny but still-standing pine. At the end of the row of buildings and separated from them by a distance of about thirty feet is a farmhouse. Simple in frame but tall and once proud. The roof is caved in, a great toothless hole gaping up at the sky.

"Nothing sadder than a roof given in, is there?" Earl asks.

"Tell me that's not where you live."

"No, ma'am. George fusses in there but I have a spot in the barn behind these buildings and down the hills that way." He points toward the saloon. "You'll love the barn. I'm fixing it up real good so a whole family could definitely live there."

Closest to us there is a firepit full of ash and blackened objects that aren't meant to burn (beer bottles, curling food wrappers, and cans). There are beer bottles strewn around the small open space. There is no sound. No birds, no crickets, no rustle of leaves. There isn't even any undergrowth. Just dusty ground that looks to have been tamped down by anxious feet. A small dead space.

"So where is he?" I've got that uh-oh feeling in my stomach. That child-molester, kidnapper, razor-blade-in-the-candy feeling: *Tell Mommy and Daddy about the bad man.*

"Where's who?" Earl asks. He is looking at me but that stupid mask makes it impossible to tell if he's joking. My eyes are tired and I'm out of breath.

"George, for fuck's sake! Where is George?" I ask,

and shiver. I zip up my jacket to my neck before crossing my arms over my chest to hug my breasts tight against my body.

"You scared?"

"No," I say, and resist the urge to ask for my pills. I've been doing some kind of something since I was sixteen, when Ray and I decided to clean up the remnants of our parents' Halloween party. Drinking, smoking, snorting. My father made me swear I would never be like him, but he only made me swear when he was sober and miserable. When he was drunk, he was happy, unafraid of the world and its consequences.

With beer or weed or speed in my system, I felt joy. It made the hate inside me shrink down. And I could forget my promise. Dad wanted me to be happy, bold, and brave. It didn't matter how I got there.

The hospital kindly turned me over to prescription drugs and life happens at arm's length now—close enough to destroy the joy and distanced enough to fog the pain. My body off of *everything* will be an unfamiliar landscape.

"Sometimes it's safer to be scared. That's what Mama says."

Maybe, I think but do not say. *Maybe feeling all of it every moment will be safer.*

Something in me shifts. Something that I thought they removed months ago opens up and I reach for him. To hug him? To shield him? My arms think better of it and drop back to my sides before I notice that he has taken a step toward me as if he knew my offer of comfort was coming before I did.

"Show me," I say.

Earl nods and leads me around the dead campfire toward the farmhouse. For a minute, I assume we are entering the building, but he lets his shoulder brush against it silently as we walk. He disappears around the corner. I pause, stand up straighter, and then step forward. There's a big man slumped in a beat-up lawn chair. His back is to me and his head is rolled slightly to one side.

Earl stops. I take a few more steps forward. I look over my shoulder at Earl, who gives me a nod.

"Hello?" The man, George, doesn't answer. I catch the smell of him as a breeze moves through. Something is wrong. Urine. Sweat. Alcohol. A darker smell too. Decay. "What's wrong with him?" I ask Earl.

"Nothing wrong with him, but I wouldn't wake him if I were you."

"Why not?" I whisper back. All the hairs on my neck are standing up.

"I'll be right back," Earl says in a quick whisper. I spin on my heels in time to see him disappear around the building.

"Goddamn it, Earl," I say, and think about following, but my legs are shaking.

George is wearing a black leather jacket and a black knit hat. I can't see much about his size or anything of his hair. He is just a big, sloppy body in a chair. From the back George could be anyone. Could be my dad. Could be Lowell. Could be Ray. Could be me.

"Do you need help?" I ask, and take a step toward the body. "Listen, your kid said you'd be able to give me gas. My van ran out. That's all I need, then I'm gone."

As I come up beside him, I have to cover my mouth and nose. The smell is strong. The hat is a ski mask. His face is invisible. Just eyes through the holes and they are open wide, a too-clear blue as if bleached out by the sky. He has on ripped jeans, which are wet from the crotch to his knees. His blue sweatshirt is slightly wet down the front. Vomit. There are beer bottles all around him. Too many to drink in one sitting. His wide eyes stare up at the tops of the trees or the sky, I can't tell which. I turn to see what he sees and two crows circle. Then a third joins and a fourth. They glide, making no noise. Their beaks sharp and ready.

"You drunk?" I study his face. He's not present, and from the looks of things, he might never even know I've been on his property. "You dead, mister?" I hadn't planned to say that word, "dead," but there it is floating around now and suddenly I know it is the obvious choice. I move toward him slowly, unsure of what I'm planning to do, but feeling sure I have to prove to myself that he isn't dead so I can leave both drunk man and small boy behind. I get close enough to reach out and tap his shoulder with two fingers. I keep my other hand clamped over my mouth and nose. No response.

I give his muddy cowboy boot a kick. Nothing.

"I wouldn't wake him up if I were you," Earl says. He's back and standing right behind me.

"God, you're a creeper. Stop sneaking up on me. If I didn't know better, I'd say this man was dead. As a matter a fact, I don't know better. He's dead. This is fucked-up."

"He's not dead. He's nappin'."

"Does he always nap with his eyes open?"

"Usually does. Yep."

"That's fucking creepy."

"He's just sleepin' it off."

"Earl, honey, he is not sleeping. Something is wrong."

"It's the white powder I gave him."

"You poisoned him?"

"It kills the rats."

I wish I could see Earl's face behind the mask. As it is, I can't tell if he's smiling or frowning and the mask has regained its glare, its crow-attracting shine. I'm close enough to him to see the hills and valleys of the tinfoil crinkles and it looks like the surface of the moon.

"Earl, I hope he's a son of a bitch."

"He's just nappin'," Earl whispers.

"How long has he been napping?"

"Since yesterday noon. I gave him some of your medicine this morning."

"How much?"

"Many of them."

"That's not a number."

"All?"

"Is he still breathing?"

"Yes, watch."

We stand quietly waiting until George's chest rises ever so slightly.

"I guess that was a breath. If he's alive, you have to get him to a doctor, and really, it strikes me as a very bad habit to be poisoning people so early in life. Just look at him. We need to call someone. I mean, *you* need to call someone."

"There isn't a phone here."

"You need to get him help before this turns into something even bigger than you want. Believe me. I know. Some choices can't be undone."

Earl is quiet for a moment, thoughtful, but then he speaks with a sadness that seems deliberate: "I was hoping you'd help me bury him."

FIVE

Earl reaches out and wraps his hand around mine. His chapped fingers press into my road-burned flesh.

There's an insistence in Earl's grip, a pleading little tug that reminds me of when I thought I had Ray's baby in me. It was only for eight weeks, but it was there, in our minds, forming its own little brain and heart, changing all of our plans. Ray sang to it. Hummed indie rock into my belly button while I read him the classified ads for Airstreams made after 1960 but before 1975.

"We'll be gypsies, Emma My Emma. We'll buy an old RV for the whole family and never stop moving."

Before Pea Baby, we talked about hitching cross-country. Stopping at the most desolate places we could imagine: the Petrified Forest, White Sands, inner city Detroit, and always ending in the Badlands where we'd jump off the edge of the world together. It was a suicide pact of sorts, but I honestly don't know if we meant it, because Pea Baby came along and made us talk about the world in a new way. Lush and full with plenty of places to call home. We would buy something with an eight-cylinder engine to drag our living space behind us. The Badlands would just be another stop and perhaps I'd accept that scholarship I'd earned to Antioch College and we'd stay there awhile before moving on.

Ray had layers of secret lives. I called him the Everlasting Gobstopper, or Gobs for short. Red on the outside then yellow then orange then white. Emma and Ray forever was the solid white center. I was Queen of the White Core where we loved each other in a way no one would understand.

There were darker layers than the ones he shared with me. I knew that. But then there was the hope. The possible happy ending. Pea Baby.

Earl's little hand and Pea Baby have a lot in common—their weight fleeting and precious.

"Please," he says, all little-boy quiet. "I need to make him go away."

"Let's get something straight right now," I say, and pry my hand out of his. "This dude is not my problem and neither are you. And I don't like to be touched. Please remember that."

"Just do the last bit for me and this will be my land. My home."

The farmhouse is behind me. Its cellar door in my peripheral vision. One metal door swung open, one closed. The dark hole of a mouth is ready to vomit up the horrid history of this place. *George could be dumped down those stairs. Tipped out of his lawn chair and kept out of sight.*

Earl, as if inside my head, moves to the side of the house and sits himself down so that his back rests against the splintery clapboard just to the left of the coffin I've imagined for George. I turn away from George to face Earl and the house. The rich dark of that cellar. The invitation of it is delicious.

When we were finally alone, and I'd stopped crying long enough to tell him it wasn't a baby I was carrying, but a tumor—baby shaped, perhaps, but a tumor all the same—Ray said, "We'll go back to the plan. Jump off the edge of a deep, dark something and then burrow underground until the earth blankets us. You, me, and tumor baby."

"Jesus, Earl."

"What?"

"I just need gas," I say, thinking, *And medication.* "That's all I'm here for. I can send someone out to help when I get where I'm going."

Earl tips his face to the ground, then whispers, "That's not your van down there."

"Excuse me?"

"It's. Not. Yours."

"It is now." I turn my back to Earl and take in the forest beyond George. The tall, proud spruce trees are thick here behind the row of buildings. There is a stream nearby. The sound is light and thin, but it leads to the river that runs through the base of these hills.

"I looked at the papers in the glove box. They don't say *you.*"

"How did you get in? I locked her up."

"I know how to jimmy locks," he says, so proud of himself that I feel proud of him too. "Also, I stole your keys."

"Give them back." I spin to look at him. He's sitting now, Indian style, against the building. The mask big and bright and caught up on the collar of his shirt so that it sits crooked on his face.

"I'll give 'em back," he says, but he does not move to do so. "Lowell Smith," he says.

"Excuse me?"

"It's his van. I also found a picture of a little girl and her mama." Earl pulls out a wallet-size photo and holds it out toward me. I haven't seen this photo before. The little girl is beautiful. Her grin big, her blond hair blowing around her face. Her mother kneeling down behind her to rest her own big smile over her daughter's shoulder. *Fuck you, Lowell*, I think. *Good riddance.* I make no move to take it so Earl puts the photo back in his pocket. "They love each other. They are a sweet family."

"Lowell's a fucking asshole," I say. "I mean, not a nice guy."

"Oh, I know tons of curse words," he says proudly. "You want to hear them? I know asshole and shit and hell and dermit and fuck." He whispers the f-word.

"Dermit is not a curse word."

"But it's not *good*." He nods so sincerely that I smile.

"You're right. It's not good." A cold wind rushes the patch of land I stand on, pulling tangled strands of hair across my face.

"So you'll help, right? I'll get gas and give Lowell's keys back and you'll help me."

"Earl, *I'm* not a good guy. Don't assume anyone is. Even if I wanted to help you, you shouldn't accept my help. Good things don't happen around me."

"George has money in his back pocket. A *lot* of money."

"All I need is gas. That's it."

"Can you get the money for me?"

"Why can't you get it yourself?"

He shrugs.

I study George, a hulking mass of a man in a shitty lawn chair.

"If you're too scared, I understand," he says.

On his eighteenth birthday, Ray and I had a fight. I don't remember what we said. I don't want to remember what *I* said. Though it's getting harder without the layer of drugs in my system to hold up the curtain between now and then.

I do remember that I called Ray a cocksucker and that I wanted to shake him. Wrap my hands around his biceps until my fingertips sank deep bruises into his skin and his neck either snapped or he decided to fight back, kick me on my ass, claw himself free, scream out what he really thought of me. Instead I shoved him in the chest and called him that name. He looked shocked, stunned really, but then he reached out and grabbed me by the arms just as I'd thought I might do to him. Instead of shaking me, he kissed me. On the lips. So hard that we clanked teeth and I could taste blood in my mouth. The affection between us was always too intimate for siblings, but we weren't lovers. Even though I wanted to be. Not until that night. I was a virgin. He wasn't. I know that now. We both assumed he'd gotten me pregnant when my period stopped and my belly gained a strange firm grapefruit of roundness. The one time we crossed the line and it was angry and painful and the end of so many things. He disappeared for a few days after that. He walked out of the house and didn't come back. I was so scared of what we'd done. Terrified I'd never see him again. Terrified I *would* see him again and that I'd disgust him as much as I disgusted myself.

"I'm not scared," I say to Earl.

I walk up to stand in front of George. His breath comes slow and labored. I grab up one of his stiff arms, pull him forward so he just about falls out of his seat and reach around to his jeans pocket where a wad of money is suddenly perfectly visible. I pull it out easily. I check his other back pocket. Nothing. I toss the money to Earl and let the body flop in half as I walk around the farmhouse and away from his ghost town.

"I'm sorry, Emma. Please don't go." His voice is pulling at me even before he is tugging at the back of my jacket. "You can have some of the money."

"Earl, I can't help you. I have too many problems of my own."

"You can have all the money, Emma. All of it! We can live together. I'll sign over the deed to you and everything." Something hits my back, a soft thump. I stop, stand still even as the hill slopes downward under my feet. The cash he threw at my back is on the ground. I could pull loose. I could keep moving but I don't. I look at him, planting my feet firmly.

"Let me see your face."

"No."

"Why not?"

"I don't show people. Not any people."

"Show them what?" I ask, but he does not answer. He tightens his lips into a white line. "I don't trust you, Earl."

"That's okay. I don't trust anyone either."

"That's sad."

"Where are you going?"

"I'm going to the Badlands."

"But you need gas. And medicine. My mom has pills. Maybe they are the same. I'll give you some."

"No, I'm done with pills, and I'll hitch," I say, but I'm lying about both things. I can't leave Veronica here, and if handed a pill I'd surely swallow it. "Besides, there must be someone else out here. There is no way you are out here all on your own."

"Please, Emma." He's shaking. His eyes wet and full, spilling over behind the mask. "Stay with me. Or don't go right away. Just be here a little while."

"I can't take care of you, Earl." This is the understatement of the year, but there is a positive pitch to my voice that I didn't intend. He brightens. Smiles up at me.

"I don't need taking care of. I just need company."

"Earl, honey, I'm not suggesting you need someone to change your diapers, but someone clearly needs to be looking after you. Do you ever take that mask off or do you wear it to bed?"

He doesn't answer.

"You do, don't you? You wear it to bed," I say. "Okay. Tell me one other thing. What were you planning to do with George before I came along?"

"The crows. I thought they'd eat him," Earl says, face to the ground. "They usually only like strong things. Still alive things. I didn't let him die all the way so they might still eat him but they haven't yet."

"You're lying."

"Can I show you my town? Maybe we'll find gas. George has a lot of supplies, and if he's dead, they belong to me. I can give you what you want. Just promise to help me get rid of George before you go."

Veronica is down in that parking lot. She has no gas. She will not run, and I will not run without her. I need to find gas.

"My mother didn't want to leave me," Earl says. "She wanted to stay and make this place good."

"Sometimes people disappoint you," I say.

"He killed her. Choked the air out of her and then put her body in the cellar. It's okay though. She's not really down there. She turned before he dropped her down the stairs."

"Don't say 'turned' like she's some kind of zombie."

"You don't know how it is here."

"I know that your mother left you with that horrible man."

We face each other. The woods are quiet. The air feels colder and heavier than before. Snow is coming.

"Jesus, Earl." He's standing as still as one of the spruce trees surrounding us. "I didn't mean to say that."

"He was still alive when she turned."

Earl flops to the ground and pulls his knees up under his chin.

"I fed her soul to the crows," Earl whispers. "She's one of 'em now," he says, and on cue, I hear the birds calling to each other, circling nearby.

"Bullshit," I say. "Get up, Earl." He doesn't move. I

feel suddenly angry. "Get the fuck up off the ground. Everything you say is bullshit." I reach out and put my hands on him, my arms on his shoulders, and he reacts quickly, shoving me so I rock back onto my ass.

"She was gonna kill him but he got to her first and now she's up there."

"What the fuck are you talking about, Earl? Who's up where?"

"My mama keeps track of me when she's not in her old body. The one in the cellar." He holds his face up to the sky and the sun glints and flashes off the mask. He keeps his face up and holds his arms out, waiting, but for what? And then I hear them, the wild pterodactyl cry of those fucking crows.

"Is that why you wear that stupid mask? For the crows?"

"I made it," he says, and I realize I've insulted him.

"It is beautiful. Your art is actually pretty amazing."

He smiles so wide that his cheekbones push his mask up on his face.

I'm staring up at his shiny mask with his green, green eyes peeking out at me.

"No parent should ever leave their kid," I say, thinking maybe I can trip him up and get him to admit she's not actually dead.

"She couldn't help it. And she'll come back. She promised. For real come back. Like she was when she was my mama," he mumbles. "I just have to wait for her so she can find herself again."

"Can I get this straight for a second?"

He shrugs his *Sure, why not?*

"Your father killed your mother. Her body is in the cellar, but you think her soul has entered a crow and will stay in that crow until she can find a way back to her body?"

"Yes," he says. Succinct and pleased with himself.

"That all sounds highly unlikely."

"It does," he says, sounding even more pleased with himself. As if unique circumstances shape an opportunity for pride no matter what the nature of those circumstances are.

I let the silence rest between us for a while. What would be the harm of driving him out of here? I could leave him at a campground or at a National Park office. Either would be better than here.

"Fine, Earl. Help me find gas and we'll both get out of here."

"Oh, I could never leave. You stay!"

"I'm not staying here, Earl. I would never stay here, but I'm saying I'll take you out of here and get you someplace safe. It's a good offer. You should take it."

"I don't want to leave. Plus, we can't leave tonight."

"And why is that?"

"It's gonna snow. A bad snow," he says, and a pristine

white flake rests for a second on his shoulders before it melts.

"Okay. I'll leave tomorrow if I have to. You can come with or stay. You're really not my problem." I stand and brush off the back of my pants. "But let's find the gas for Veronica."

"Who's Veronica?"

"The van. I named the van." I blush a little.

"George's truck is in my barn. It might still have gas!" He is excited, as if this has only just occurred to him. A lie of omission. He's known all along there was a vehicle in these hills. "I can show you where I stay. I have a stove. We'll be warm there tonight or for forever if you stay."

Earl looks down, picks at his pants with his thumb and forefinger. His hair springs up wild at the top of his head behind the mask.

"Earl, honey, I can't even take care of myself."

"I'm scared," he says, and I see that he is. "Please don't leave me," he says.

"I'm not helping you bury that man alive," I say softly.

"But if he dies, like really dies dead, you'll help, right? You will, won't you? Maybe then you'll stay."

"I won't stay. No means no on that one, Earl, but I'll stay a bit. *Not* to see what you think is so great about this place, but because I need gas and a place to sleep tonight."

"Thank you, Emma! Thank you!"

"I just said I'd stay the night. That's it."

"Okay," he says. He can barely stand still he's so happy.

"George needs medical attention, Earl. You've got to get him help. Once I leave, I'm going to have to tell the cops that you need help. They can get George to the hospital. They can find you a home."

"I have a home, but you do what you have to. I'm not worried about that."

"Earl. It's going to snow tonight. George'll be dead by morning if we leave him in that chair. And no one is ever going to leave you alone if they think you're a murderer. Not ever."

"Maybe you can take George with you when you go? Get him to a hospital for me."

"Whoa," I say with my hands out in front of me. "That's a big ask."

"You could just move him inside for me. It stays warmer in the house. He won't die all the way and then you can take him to the hospital and he'll probably die there or on the way there. That way we get to try to save him *and* we get rid of him all at the same time." He claps his hands together with glee, as if he alone has just solved the problem of world peace. "Just tilt him down the stairs."

"I'm not lugging around a dead body." I'm thinking of the truck he claims to have. How much gas might it have? Will I be able to siphon it? Could I drive it straight to Veronica? "I don't want to waste any more time on you than I already have. I'm sorry if that sounds harsh, but . . ."

"I'll tell them about you," Earl says in a whisper.

"Excuse me?"

"I'll tell the police that you were here. I'll tell them what you did."

"What did I do?"

"You stole a van. You poisoned George with your medicine. You hurt my face."

I study him. The snow falls faster. I'm shaking and hungry. The wind is picking up force. It tugs at me, eating at the stitching of my jacket to worm its way inside.

"You wouldn't."

"I would."

I am far less worried about Earl's hollow threats than I am about surviving this weather and whatever my suddenly sober body will put me through. He can't hurt me if we never make it out of these hills.

"I have gas."

"How long will it take to get the gas and get back to Veronica?"

"A few hours," Earl says.

"A few hours! Where is this stupid truck?"

"I have a few things I want to get to show you. They are supercool and you might think differently about this place if you see them all."

"What stuff could you possibly have?"

"My art."

"Okay. We are staying together and the goal is the truck and even if you are the most amazing artist ever,

I'm getting out of here first thing tomorrow. We are not separating. You need to let that idea go."

"I'll meet you here in just a second and then we can go to the barn for the truck."

"No," I say, meaning, we are not playing games, we are getting to that barn to see the truck and then we can stay warm until morning while I think through my next steps. "We will do all of this now and we will do it together."

"I love you, Emma," Earl says suddenly, and out of the blue, and before I know what's what, he's thrown his little arms around me. His masked head pressing up against the underside of my breasts is rigid. I stand surprised with my arms raised above my head for a minute, but he doesn't let go. *So much for not touching.* "I'll convince you to stay. I know I will." And suddenly he is moving again, taking big steps downhill and starting to run.

"Earl!" I yell, but I don't sound confident and Earl doesn't stop. He's gone. I'm alone.

He loves me, I think. He doesn't love me. He doesn't even know me. Then again, I never really knew Ray. We used to love being in physical contact, piled up on each other like puppies. I knew every freckle. All his ticklish spots. Exactly what he smelled like at every time of day. Siamese twins we were, and even with all that, I didn't *know* him, but I loved him.

I turn around and head back uphill to George. At the flat of the hill, I stop to catch my breath. I scan the land.

A strong breeze rushes past and carries George's smell with it, reassuring me that he is still there. I hear my name from downhill where Earl has disappeared. I spin, do a pirouette scan of the woods, but there is only the house and, presumably, George beyond it.

"Earl?" I ask the hilltop. It is only ten steps to where George is, slouched over and gruesome in his stupid lawn chair. I make my way around to stand in front of him.

I pull the gun out of my pocket and open the barrel. There are no bullets left, the ones Earl shot were the last. It's a harmless object now but no one has to know that. If George suddenly pops back to life, I can keep him at a distance.

The lawn chair has a metal frame, but the seat and back are made of long strips of yellow plastic that have molded around George's ass.

I walk around to face slumped-over George. I zip my jacket up to my throat and take a deep breath of clean air. I will thread my arms under his armpits so that I can lift him and drag him to the house. The front door. Not the cellar. He probably won't live much longer inside than out, but it doesn't seem right to leave him in the cold.

I step up.

Be brave.

I move in a little closer so I can tilt him back and look at his eyes. I will take his ski mask off. That will make him human. With my hand on the knit, I pull it up to uncover his lips and with them a low growl, barely a squeak, wrenches free of his body and drops spit onto his lips and my fingers.

"Shit," I say, and stumble backward to fall hard on my tailbone. George stays upright, his lips still exposed to the fresh air. I stare at him, the sideshow attraction, as his head lolls left and then right. His eyes blink shut and then open. Shut. Open. I see his eyeballs moistening and focusing. He sees me.

"Help," he whispers. Gut ripped. "Get help."

SIX

I watch George from the ground. A huge man in a too-small chair, he has a broad chest and a neck too thick for his head. Earl has made him a temporary rag doll, his limbs too heavy to move, but if he comes around to his full force, I will be in trouble.

"Do you hear that?" George asks. His head lolls back on his neck so loose and sloppy that I fear it will fall off and bounce away into the hungry darkness of the cellar behind him. With great effort, he rights his head on his shoulders. Drool slips from the corner of his mouth and glistens in the scruff of his graying beard.

"Hear what?" I ask.

"That bitch is here," he says. "I hear you!" he screams into the woods, and for a brief moment, the cords of his neck stand out thick and red. Fierce as tree trunks. His chin falls to his chest, the black ski mask still covering his brow.

George mumbles something.

"Excuse me?"

"I hear her out there. She thinks I don't know she's lurking. That I won't catch her."

"Jesus Christ," I whisper.

"I can't move my body."

"I see that and I'm grateful."

He chuckles.

The wind blows past him and toward me. I cover my nose with my hand. His piss smell is strong, fresh even.

"Why are you bloody?" he asks.

"I fell. I need to wash up."

"Stream's just behind the storefront. No one's stopping you," he says. "Hear that? Do you hear that?!"

"I don't hear anything."

"She whistles all the time. Same stupid song."

I listen hard but hear nothing human, only the stream George mentioned and the wind as it moves through the loose planks of the house behind us.

"I need some gas to get out of here, and if I can get that, I'll call for help for you as soon as I'm able."

"You've got to stab her right in the heart. Then burn this place down. That's the plan."

"Whose plan?" I ask.

"My plan!" he yells, and smacks his hand to his chest.

The thump is strong even as his arm falls heavily back into his lap and stays there thick as a log.

"Get the insurance money. Fuck me if she's gonna do it first. It was my idea."

"Is someone else out here? Besides you and me and Earl?" I ask.

"Earl?" he asks, and then scoffs. "Wait, did you bring me more? Tell me there aren't any more now."

"More what?"

He shifts his feet on the ground. He'll be mobile soon. The poison, the meds, whatever else Earl's given him is wearing off.

I jump up.

"Hey!" he hollers after me.

I run around the farmhouse to look at the storefronts and the long porch that connects the buildings. It stretches out like piano keys. Some planks are missing, others rest where asked, but spit up their nails in protest.

The door of the dime store is painted bright red and newly so. It isn't peeling in the way that the other doors look to be and there is a fresh piece of glass in the frame. It is thick, double paned, and crystal clear.

The red door opens easily. The space inside is set up like one might expect it to be if this were a movie set. The counter is on my left, an old cash register sits on top. Shoulder-height shelving lines the room and the shelves behind the counter are full with small wooden bins. The bins are empty, but they would fill quite easily with candy and gum and cigarettes. Everything is made of pine and the shelves are carefully constructed, newly fitted to the wall.

I exit the dime store and push open the door of the grocery store. The space is twice as big and has not been touched. It is largely empty with dust coating the floor. Sun rushes in through a hole in the back wall. On the floor near me is a toolbox with very little dust on top. I squat down and open its lid, hammers and screwdrivers, pliers. I pull out the drawers, three of them, one at a time. My heart pounding. Nails and Allen wrenches and green garden twine. I jog back out to George, who sits as I left him in the lawn chair. He's passed out again.

I twine his right wrist to the chair. I wrap it around and around as tight as I can before I move to his other hand, using the twine to keep his right wrist and hand connected to the chair. If he regains his full strength, mentally and/or physically, he will easily get out. I know that. This is a small reassurance that I can keep track of him, and in his weakened state, he might actually stay put.

He rustles a bit and my heart hammers faster. I pull tighter on the twine, make sure it cuts into his skin, not drawing blood but if he fights it will. When I am done, I step back, feeling confident.

The wind picks up and with it the whistle George promised. The sound of it whipping through the wood of the farmhouse, dipping into the gaping hole in the roof and rushing to find its way out of smaller cracks and crevices. The open cellar door shudders and then slams shut. My shoulders jump up around my ears but George doesn't move.

Could I drag man and lawn chair into the house? Would that convince anyone that I'd tried to save him?

"Why'd you go and do that?" he asks, barely waking.

I shriek, a small animal noise, like a rabbit. Clearing my throat and deepening my voice, I say, "Your son says you're dangerous."

"I don't have a son." He slurs his words and the slurring seems to make him giggle.

"Well, I'm sure he'd rather not claim you either, but he's real enough. You need to tell me if I can find gas on this property."

"Hell, yes, you can find gas. Loads of it. Enough to blow the whole place up." He giggles. "Take this ski mask off my forehead. Itches."

I don't want to touch him or go too near, but he's still weak and I'd like to see his full face.

I move behind him and reach out from arm's length to pull the mask off.

The relief of it gone seems to make him pass out again. His head hangs forward. There is a tattoo on the back of his neck. Three black lines. Wavy. Like water.

"What is this place exactly?" I ask.

"It's my fucking freak show. My goddamn fresh start. Can't you tell?"

"I don't mean what is it to you. I mean why is it here."

"It's an old mining town. They thought they'd found gold and maybe they did but not much. Mostly they found metals like copper. But all that dried up a long time ago. The 1940s. That house there. *My* house belonged to the mine manager. They say he hung himself inside when he realized there wasn't enough to keep the place going. I thought I could make money back off this place. I probably could have if my fucking family had just listened to me. Come to think of it that's probably what he thought too. They say he killed his men. Lined 'em up on payday and shot them. Got the first one in the head but the others weren't so easy. Started moving and had to hunt them in these woods."

"You don't seem much better."

"You think this place isn't evil? You think I had a choice? This place is hungry and fuck you anyway. Now leave me be," he says. "I'm tired."

"You're drugged," I say, but he's already gone under again. I smell the ski mask. It's not terrible so I shove it in my pocket.

I look around me at the back of this almost town. None of it belongs here, yet it's all stubbornly built to outlast its own story. Its ghostly outline too weak for human life and too strong for the hills to reclaim.

The closed cellar doors make me feel brave. I walk around George to the front of the house and climb the three steps to the porch. Like the storefronts, the house is deteriorating with only a few signs that anyone is trying to fight it. The front door is shut, a solid door, made of the same pine that built this miniature city.

Inside the house the air moves, whirls and runs and rushes in little eddies. Snow floats by in the darkened front room to my left, catching the sunlight that floods in with it from the hole in the roof. The flakes shine and fall to dust the floor, sparkle their bright icicle selves and rest without melting. I cross my arms under my breasts so my leather jacket hugs tighter to my body. In front of me is a straight and sturdy staircase leading to the second floor and, to the right of the stairs, a hallway lined with an Oriental rug—its gold and blues still fairly vibrant in the old dark of the house. An upright piano sits in the room to the right along with a sofa covered with a white sheet and piles of moving boxes.

The piano room is shadowed, dark in the corners. The floorboards groan. There is a cellar down there. Its depth and body count undetermined. I step as lightly as I can. The space adjusts to my presence. It wheezes and splinters.

The boxes are stacked around a double mattress on the floor, probably to protect the person sleeping there from the rush of the wind whipping through the hole of a house. The bedsheets are tousled, its blankets too few for winter.

George sleeps here, I think. A space heater sits at the open foot of the bed.

"There's a generator," I say. I move to a floor lamp and switch it on.

The boxes are neatly labeled. A woman's handwriting: *kitchen*, *bathroom*, *keepsakes*. And then a little kid's hand: *toyz*, *books*, *stuff*. I open a few and find their contents true to their labels. The one marked *closet* is full of clothes. Dresses, shirts, T-shirts with puppies a kid's size five. A little girl. I hold a small pink shirt to my nose and remember a similar shirt I had when I was little. Pink with white cuffs and a strawberry on the front. I loved that shirt. This one, saved, I imagine, by Earl's mother, smells of the box and of its travels—like baby powder sprinkled through a horse stable. Sweet and fecal at the same time.

I pull the box that reads *keepsakes* off the top of a stack of three large boxes and it smacks the floorboards. The floor stays intact. Unfolding the lid, I find photographs. Not old-timey enough for a ghost town. More recent than that. Polaroids of a man and a woman. The man is some long-gone version of George. Shaved and smiling. Not yet an evil thing. The woman is beautiful. Young. Long, blond hair with big sunglasses above high cheekbones. A baby in her arms. There are lots of her and the baby. Packets of them with their negatives still in their sleeves. The baby is fat cheeked and held close. There are only a few pictures like this of me with my mom and dad. The three of us looking like a family. I always blamed my mom for not having more photos of us, but now that seems cruel. We kept having to move and in each move something else would go, but my father always made sure I had my stuffed tiger, Clover, so I thought he was a hero. I never thought about all the other things he let slip away.

I push the box aside.

What am I even looking for? I need gasoline. That's the only thing I need from this place.

Outside the wind has picked up. It's cold, especially in the shade of the porch. The gun presses into my torso.

"George," I say, walking back to stand in front of him. He does not answer. His eyes are closed, head drooping forward. My makeshift ties look silly, crafty rather than professional against his thick wrists. "Wake up," I say, and kick his foot.

I take the gun out of my pocket and knock it against his cheek. His eyes flutter open. He sees what I intend for him to see and then lets his head fall to his chest again.

"Where is the gas?"

"I don't fucking feel right," he says, and starts coughing. The cough starts up front and then comes from someplace deeper. White foam comes up next, onto his chest, his head resting heavily against his breastbone as he coughs.

"You all right?" I ask, but the retching gets worse, moves through his body, and for a moment, he pulls at the ties I've put on his arms and they give a little but not enough. He slams his feet into the dry brush and his chair tips, he goes backward and is on his back, gagging.

I rush forward and pull on the arm of the chair. Something snaps and I move my hands to his arm, grabbing cloth. I can't pull him over so I move to the other side and push.

Chair and George tip onto their sides. He continues to vomit but now it's clearing his throat.

I step back and let him go. It takes a while for him to quiet.

"Undo my hands," he says.

"No."

"Check the cellar," he says. "For supplies."

"Fuck you."

He laughs.

I look to the now-closed cellar doors.

"Why would you keep the gas in the cellar?"

"Flashlight in the toolbox. I resting now," he says into the cold ground and then he passes out again.

"I'm not going in the cellar," I say to no one, but then I'm walking back to the storefronts, peering in windows at empty rooms and finding nothing inside.

In the grocery store, I dig through the tools and find a heavy-duty flashlight. The batteries are still good.

I give George a kick in the boot as I pass. He doesn't move.

"I'm going to check the cellar," I say. He says nothing. I watch carefully. His breath moves a blade of grass near his nose. Not dead yet.

I set down the flashlight to open both doors. One, then the other, and they creak open wide. The smell of earth comes up warm into the cold October air. The depth of the darkness seems unreal, swallowing everything but the top three steps.

Behind me the wind blows, harder suddenly, as if desperate to push me into the black hole of a cellar. I smell George on the wind. All his stink has exited his body, fleeing the scene of him. The earth too stubborn to absorb any more human waste.

The smell of George, the cold, and the feel of the ghost town watching make the cellar less terrifying or at least turn it into a simple extension of the horror show I'm already in. It's just a hole in the ground, dug by a man who wanted to make a home. A cellar could have hope in it.

The darkness parts for the beam of the flashlight. I will only need to take a step or two inside to see if there is any truth to what George has told me. There will either be something there or there won't.

I put both boots on the first step. It's sturdier than the floor of the house. The second step. Solid. Third. The walls are dirt, roots poke out into the dark, veiny and pale. The ceiling is low and the beams even lower.

I no longer smell George. Instead, I smell the earth.

Rich and thick. I point the beam of the flashlight to the floor and water reflects up at me. Just a shallow layer that has not soaked in. A recent rain. There is a table against a far wall with cardboard boxes stacked on top. One of them says *kitchen* and another says *magazines*.

Breaking my promise to myself to not go in too far, I step down into the water. It's not deep but it's thick, more mud than water. My boots make a sucking sound when I lift my feet.

I reach my hand out and touch a box. The exterior gives under pressure like flesh and then my fingers slide through, touching something that feels like fur.

The room changes. The warmth, the earthen smell unsafe. The house above me creaking as it thinks about collapse. How could Earl want to stay here?

There is a smaller space back behind the chimney. The walls are wet with mud. I trip over nothing but lose my balance anyway and dig the fingers of my right hand into the wall to keep from falling to the floor. Once balanced I pull my hand from the muck and wipe it on my blood-stained jeans.

I should not be down here.

I walk forward and touch the brick of the chimney. I hold my place while I point the beam beyond it into a dark cavern of a room. A wooden dining chair sits in the corner. The cane of the seating punctured through by years of people sitting in it. If I stay too long my brain will fill that chair.

My mind stores bits of horror in places only it can call up to use against me. Bodies that have cracked open, skin that bubbles and churns. Liquids that ooze and morph, skitter and squirrel themselves back into human form and then sit themselves lumpy in a chair across from me in a dark, dark basement. There she is, looking just like me, Emma My Emma, belly gaping open, joints bent at the wrong angles, hairs wiggling along her arms like worms.

"We are all of us made up of crazy," Ray liked to say. "And madness in its simplest form is narcissism—a self stared at so long and so hard that any potential beauty in it becomes horrifying."

The flashlight beam captures gas cans in the far corner. Three of them. George was not lying. A blip of hope. It's possible that life is a series of steps. You take one and then another and then another until you are on a journey. You have purpose. Control.

I move toward the chair and the gas cans behind it, but I stop short. Maybe it's the still empty chair facing me or the beer bottles at its base that make me turn around to see what I would see if I sat in the chair. And there she is, the body. The inevitable ghost in the ghost-town cellar.

An unerasable thing.

She's been there a long time and if she still has a smell its indistinguishable from the damp rot of the cellar itself. She sits propped against the chimney. Her hands are in her lap. Her chin somehow still held high to look back at the chair. Defiant. Her skin is leathery, shrunken, her bones too large to be kept inside by what's left of her outer layers. Cheekbones push through, a glaring white.

The beam fades slowly, going from bright to nothing in the time it takes for me to realize how dark it will be without it right before it goes. I shake it, slap it on my thigh, but it stays stubbornly out. The chair behind me begins to fill. The softened wood of the collapsed cane seat working to hold someone up. The creak of the body nestling in. I drop the flashlight into the mud, it makes a soft sploosh and I dig through my pockets for my Zippo. I wrap my fingers around the metal and pull it out of my pocket. Flick it once, twice. It doesn't light. The exhale of breath comes into the room. Alcohol. Hate. Secrets. The Zippo lights. I see him then in the chair. My daddy. Elbows on knees. Hands to face. In the weak light, he raises his face to me, and I see his eyelids black and leathery like a crow's. He blinks rapidly in the faint light.

"The train's coming," he says. "Choo choooo."

I step backward from his ridiculous grin. His impossible body leaning back in the chair so that it tilts on two legs. I step on her. On Earl's mother and I fall backward. Land in her lap, my nose to her neck as if I want her to cradle me and she is soft, warm. Her flesh full. She smells good, like sandalwood and something softer, baby powder. For a second there is still light and so I imagine her arms rise up to wrap me in a hug. She holds on to me and I feel it all—the love she has left in her. We are there in it together before I feel it turn to sadness. It isn't me she wants.

"Get the baby. She's in the corner."

I hear it crying before I know Ray is in the dark, holding her, our little nothing. Our never-real baby. Crying loud and clear and terrified. The room fills with Ray's smell and his voice: "Emma, you were supposed to come with us."

And then there's fear.

The murk of the cellar floor lets the flame live for a second, maybe two. A cellar door slams. The flame is snuffed out. The second cellar door slams. It is pitch-black.

I launch myself up as part of her loosens under my weight. Detaches. I hear skin, what's left of it, separate from the whole of her. An arm, maybe. Some appendage she does not need. I'm around the chimney and finding the stairs with my feet in an instant. The miracle of adrenaline making me both fast and efficient.

I push the cellar doors open wide, one with each hand and hurl myself into the fading daylight.

I throw up then. Vomit canned beans and stomach juices until nothing else comes up.

On my hands and knees, I try to breathe. My abdomen sore, my throat burning. For a second, I think I'll shit myself. I don't. Then I hear the whistling. Long and low. Directed into a tune I can't recognize. I raise my head and there is the lawn chair, righted so it sits facing the cellar. Empty. George is gone. The green twine I used to tie him up still tangled around the armrest of the chair.

I rise. I need to get out. I run into the wood, wheezing in the cold air.

In the distance, I hear a train. The click and clack of it on the tracks.

SEVEN

Everything looks familiar and nothing looks familiar. My heart continues to thump and I stumble forward, trip over roots, and reach out to catch myself on tree trunks that rub at my already raw palm. I need to slow down and think. The snow is falling again and starting to stick.

I stop on flat ground. I bend at my knees and hang my head low.

Breathe, Emma. I'm light-headed. Hyperventilating. *In. Out. In. Out. It's not so fucking bad, Emma.*

It starts to come back. Some breath. Some sense. Earl's mother's body is down there. She's been dead awhile. Earl told me as much in his own way. At least

George didn't eat her or feed her to the crows or whatever. This is better, right? She's just dead. Not chopped up. Not digested. Dead and underground where a good body should be. I stand up straight, press my back to a tall pine. I'm steadier, but I'm shivering. I can't stop shaking and even trying to stop seems to make it worse. *George killed her and he'll kill you next*, a little voice in my head is whispering. *He shoved her down those stairs and shut the door. Maybe she wasn't even dead when he shut the doors. Maybe it took days. Maybe Earl could have saved her and he didn't.*

"Shut up," I say to myself aloud. "The world is full of fucked-up shit. I just need to get to the end of it."

I shut my eyes and picture the Badlands the way Ray and I always did. Red and craggy. Stretching out before us. Our toes on the edge of a dusty cliff. Our arms out at our sides. Ready to fly.

I open my eyes slowly to the wintry world right here. All around me things are beginning to change. The pines are preparing to carry more weight, puffing up their needles and shaking off their branches. Snow blankets the cold skin of the boulders that dot the landscape. A flake catches on my eyelashes, accidental, and another on my tongue, purposeful. They melt a cold softness. I blink to keep the flakes off of my eyeballs. They land burning kisses on my cheeks, my forehead, and my throat. The flakes gain an icy weight, turn into pebbles that push down to meet ground.

I'm in a fairy tale: *The Big-Breasted, Blood-Encrusted Princess.*

"Once upon a time there was a dark-haired girl who liked to eat snow and run away from dead bodies," I say to no one.

Think, Emma.

Which direction is the diner? I walked uphill with Earl so I simply need to head down, but down no longer looks like one simple direction. Snow swirls through the gaps in the trees and a multitude of foggy white paths appear. Were there always so many ways to twist through these trees? Adrenaline takes ahold of the back of my neck and burns through the muscles in my shoulders. It doesn't matter. I will find the diner and the parking lot when the land levels out. I tell myself this is true. I can't have gone that far off the trail Earl led me up. I move, picking up my thick feet as quickly as I can. The snow is falling fast and the terrain is unrecognizable. It's disorienting, like I've been spinning myself dizzy, and yet every individual flake and tree and root remains in focus. All I can see is white, and the shaking is taking hold of my hands and teeth. My shoulder hits a tree trunk, stopping me in my tracks, and my feet slide ahead of me. My ass hits the ground. The wind is whipping at me and urging me to stop. It lashes around trees with that evil hint of a train whistle.

The temperature is dropping. I peer past tree trunks

to see something almost as tall as the trees, minus the bark.

Where is George? Has he gone inside to sit out the storm or is he close by, following me?

An old stone chimney juts up singularly phallic. The stones are snug, piled strong, and they lead down gracefully to an old foundation that's laid out like a game of hopscotch. I could toss and skip single footed from room to room on a better, brighter day. I kneel down, creaky kneed, to touch the skeleton of the house.

There is a chance that real families exist. One might have lived inside these walls. Newborn babies and second-floor nursery moments. Hot meals around a table. A group of people who choose each other over and over again.

I remember how angry my mom was with me after she married Frank and I wouldn't speak to him. Literally did not utter a word to him for nearly a year. She couldn't understand why I wasn't grateful. She was right to be mad. I know that now and I knew it then. She was handing me something that maybe wasn't perfect, maybe wasn't what I'd asked for, but it was a fresh start. Trying it out would not have done harm.

"Damn it, Emma. I know you miss your father, but he's gone. And honestly, he wasn't that great a dad when he was alive," she said. She shushed me when I began to protest and continued. "I don't know what you've made him into in your head, but he was always drinking. Never really present. He loved you. Please know that, but I loved you too. Still do."

She was right about some of what she said. I didn't want a new dad. Frank was boring. He watched football and went to the gym and aspired to nothing more than the purchase of a new camcorder. He bought us a house that looked like every other house. And, somehow worst of all, he loved my mom too much. More than she loved him. I could see that she was stuffing it all down to make a good choice. The right choice. So much so that she failed to notice how I was already like my father, sneaking into the kitchen to drink the last of whatever was in their glasses. I did it to impress Ray at first, but kept doing it because it felt warm and fuzzy, because it blurred the world around me into something less dangerous.

A branch snaps in the woods. The sound is sharp but the fall of it heavy, muffled by the wind and the snow already thick enough to make the ground a cushion. The falling snow is thick now too. I can see no farther than my own outstretched hands.

"Who's there?" I ask.

My mind is going to make something up. Pull the Sasquatch out of the shadows if given a chance so I look at the foundation again. There's nothing human left here. This house should never have been. The hills ate it up as fast as they could and what about the family? Settlers, surely, who never belonged here.

Our plan, Ray's and mine once we found out about

Pea Baby, was "never settle." We were going to keep moving. To give what we could, but never *claim*. "This country does not belong to us," Ray would say and I'd agree, nod my head yes, but knowing that everywhere I went, everywhere I looked, I was always looking for a home. As I found out about Pea Baby or thought I did anyway, I became one of those people Ray hated, who simply wanted a front porch and a rocking chair and someone to love them and only them. I became my mom. Pathetic.

"Earl!" I yell into the snow. "Where are you?"

I hug my jacket tighter. It isn't warm enough. The sweat I worked up in my panic is cooling, and I'm shaking more than ever. The snow pelts down, little white pills that melt before I can swallow them. George is out there somewhere. Free to find me. Free to find Earl.

"Earl!" The wind takes the name and bashes it into nearby pines.

I'll walk back, away from the ghost-root house, and I'll find the diner. I shield my eyes with my hand from the snow that's clinking against my forehead and cheeks. The sky is up there somewhere, tightened and swollen. Angry as fuck.

"Earl!" I shout. My hands are cupped around my mouth to amplify.

The dead-winter woods do nothing to answer me. I've lost feeling in my fingers and toes. The world is changing too fast, flipbook animation style all around me. My fairy tale is shifting: *Once upon a time there was a princess who slept neck-deep in a snowstorm.*

When I was Earl's age, I took in a stray cat. Fur matted and tangled. Someone had cut off all of his whiskers, leaving him to weave and bob unsure of his limitations and boundaries. I found him at the Dairy Queen and named him Avalanche. One night, I sneaked into the laundry room to dig mint-chocolate-chip ice cream out of the freezer. The next morning, no Avalanche. No purr for breakfast. No fuzzy hug. Later, I went in search of a Popsicle and found him. Peaceful, snowball curled in our freezer. I reached into cold air, fingers brushing frozen dinners and ice bags. Dead. A perfect little sculpture. He must have gone in to lick old ice cream off the side of the carton and I locked him in. My mom helped me bury him the next day. A shallow grave in the backyard that my father never noticed.

I didn't know I could set to sweating in the middle of a snowstorm, but here I am, sweating and shaking. Hypothermia or withdrawal. The only thing to do is keep walking, move my heavy feet, one, then the other. Avalanche looked so calm. So ignorant of death. My eyes keep tearing up and freezing to my lashes. I stumble forward. Trees.

My body melts first, a big gooey Emma pile falling forward through snow only because the wind is on my back. Knees hit ground, head slides forward and hits metal. Even numb fingers can tell that by some miracle

I've found the diner. A mew escapes my throat as I hoist myself up.

The air inside is warm, and my throat burns as I take my first deep breath. I stamp my boots to the floor and lightning shoots up through my knees and into my thighs. I move into the kitchen and try to light the stove but my hands are shaking. I smell gas. I try to light one match. Another. Finally, one catches and the stove puffs bright. I sink to the floor. The shaking is spreading from my hands to my arms, to my knees, even into my neck.

I let go, lie down. My clothes snow-melting to soak into the pores of my skin. I'll rest. Calm, done. The tiredness sweeps over me. Through me. The black feels so good, like velvet. I dream of Ray. His warm body is covering mine.

"I love you, Emma My Emma. Don't let anyone tell you different."

"Why didn't we stick together?" I ask. "I should have come with you."

He is running his fingers through my hair. A habit of his. He will braid it next, turn the long dark strands into puzzles and mazes. It puts me to sleep every time, this braiding game.

"It just didn't work. That's all, Emma."

"I can't remember what was supposed to happen."

"You can."

"I don't want to."

"You wanted to prove to me it was a baby."

A last-minute drug-induced revelation. My body and brain numbed by all we'd ingested. The sick, simple thought—a small incision to the belly, an opening up of the uterus. If I were to cut myself open and cup Ray's hands around the little bundle inside of me, it would swim to life.

"That's crazy," I say to Ray.

"You wanted to live. I wanted to die. It doesn't have to make more sense than that."

And then a different voice, "Shhhh."

Ray fades.

Through the darkness, I hear a series of caws and then a rattling that makes me think of a snake's long shimmer of a body, but the soft feathers that brush my skin tell me it is a crow. One of Earl's crows, I think. Talons rest on my skin, sharp needles connected by leathery toes.

"Emma," the crow says. "Emma." A bark of a name and the smooth sides of its beak brush my cheeks as if to soothe.

A wave of air that smells like cedar sweeps over me and then the crow is pulling at my limbs, taking off my wet jacket, my shoes. For a moment in my fog, I know Ray has returned just as much as I know that I am the kitten. And that's how I'd rewrite it, if I could do such a thing. I'd go back and Ray would find me in the freezer. He'd pull me out and hold me in his cupped palms, and even as I think this, I know I am confused. My mind is not right. That was before Ray. When Daddy was still alive and sleeping on the couch. In the morning, I'd change the sheets and flip the cushions so Mommy wouldn't know he'd pissed himself again.

"Daddy," I say. "Wake up." He sleeps on his side with his back to the room. His rib cage lifting toward the ceiling. His snores make him sound like he is drowning.

I shove him hard with both hands.

"Get up," I say.

"Shhhh," he says. "I have to get you warm." This is not what Daddy would say, but he's saying it as he wakes from sleep, turning toward me on the couch with his sloppy morning drool face, only his bottom half isn't turning. His torso twists separate from his pelvis, the skin stretching like Silly Putty and then the blood, oozing out of his middle.

"I'll fix it, Daddy. Just get up. I'll fix it."

"Shhhh," he says again but his face doesn't move. It's not him. I see that now. It's someone else. My father died before my ninth birthday.

"There is a body in the cellar," I say, and I see Earl's mother again. Leaning there. Her swollen skin shifts, plumping up. Her long hair turning silky. She smiles. Soft. Stands. Moves to the chair across the cellar and takes a seat. Rests her arms on her knees and leans in toward me. I fall back, rag doll on the floor. I become the body.

"I'm not good for other people," I say, but she only smiles at me with more kindness.

It comes in waves. Rolls of sick, and I retch until my body can't and then I vomit nothing. Air and regret and the memory of past consumption. I don't think it will ever stop, but then it does.

Then the world is warm and dark and soft and quiet and I go.

Darkness is replaced by a raw tenderness that prevents me from moving. My eyes are open. My joints ache, my toes burn a steady throb.

This could be dead, I think, but I move slowly, letting each appendage bend and stretch before sitting up. I'm covered in blankets I don't recognize. I'm lying next to the open oven and the kitchen is wonderfully warm. I wiggle my toes. I can feel all of them. My boots are off. My socks too. Dazed, I reach out of the blankets to touch my face and then I peek under the blankets. I'm naked except for my sports bra and underwear, and I see now that my clothes are draped over the counters. Spread out to dry. There is sick in my hair, and the smell makes me feel sick again but my stomach has nothing left to give. I wrap my hair into a tight bun at the back of my head and hold it still with an elastic.

Next to me is a lump of a little body. Hair sticking up wild from the top of the blankets. The familiar silver butterfly mask crookedly covering but not centered. It's Earl. And I realize a few things at once. First, this is my chance to see Earl's real face. Second, Earl has the body of a little girl. I think of George. *I don't have a son.*

I wrap a loose blanket around my shoulders. I lean in and try to move the mask, but Earl snorts and swats at me before rolling over on her back, the mask moving to cover more face than before. I reach for the blankets and lift them slowly, peer under. A pale body, naked except for panties. A soft waist giving in to a too-thin rib cage.

I drop the blankets back down.

I feel a sharp sadness in my chest. Was he, I mean she, so scared of me that being a boy seemed safer? Of course, it is always safer to be a boy. Everyone knows that. Fucking men always waiting to take something that isn't theirs, to reach up into your insides and tear you up.

I tiptoe around the small diner kitchen. I need time to gather my thoughts. Figure out what to do. I push open the door and step into the seating area, which is much cooler than the kitchen.

Outside the windows, the world is settling. The early morning sky is clear and bright. The snow has stopped falling. It lies thick and untouched. I hear a throat-clearing growl and a bear walks out of the trees and onto the parking lot. A big, lumbering, belly-sloppy bear sidles up to Veronica, pushing at her gently with his nose. She rocks under his weight and snow falls off her roof onto the bear's back. He shakes it off, annoyed. The snowfall has taken him by surprise as well. October, even late October, must be early for this kind of weather. He thought he had a little time before he had to hibernate. He's huge, fattened up for the winter but not yet asleep. He's crossing the snow-covered parking lot alone and leaving pothole-size footsteps behind. It's the largest animal I've ever seen. He stops and looks through the diner window to consider me the same way I am considering him. His big brown eyes are on mine. We watch each other for a moment before he moves on.

Back in the kitchen, I stand over the kid.

Our parents sent Ray on Outward Bound the year after they got married. He'd been acting out. Sneaking out of the house, cutting himself. While I managed to keep my drinking secret, Ray was not so skilled. At the wedding, my soon-to-be stepfather pulled me aside and asked me to watch out for him. He made me Ray's babysitter.

"He needs your sense of balance, Emma," his father said. "Stay close to him." Easy enough, I was already in love with Ray. Our stupid parents were so worried that they let us fall asleep, curled together in his hot room watching B movies until we slept. They saw nothing sexual between us. No warning signs at all, and perhaps they were right. Ray loved me, but not in the way I wanted him to.

My Ray was gone for three months on Outward Bound. He didn't want to go. He hated them for making him. I wrote him notes every night. Observations from the day that I would have shared with him had he been there alongside of me:

Slept through breakfast lunch and dinner. Thinking of a pizza snack. Wishing for a monkey butler.

In July, when the corn is knee high, let's fold in half and disappear.

Mrs. Hurie stopped wearing bras. Her boobs hang like pendulums when she gardens. I dare you to look away.

I had nowhere to send them, but I piled them up on loose scraps of paper and tucked them into his pillowcase.

In the end, he portaged through Minnesota in February and came back with a host of gruesome stories and a renewed love for bathroom humor and a best friend named Charlie, who I resented. Ray looked good when he came back. He'd put on weight. His cuts had healed. He loved to tell me how brave he'd been.

They jumped into icy waters on purpose so that someone else could drag them out and save them from freezing to death. You get the victim and yourself undressed, then wrap up next to them.

Earl did the same thing for me. Kept me safe. A wave of feeling passes through me right then. Protectiveness? Love? The kind of too-late feelings I should have had for Ray at the end.

My jeans are stiff, potato-bag harsh against my bruised legs. My socks are still wet, but I haven't been this well cared for since I was very little and I hadn't yet taught my mom to be afraid to love me.

Earl's clothes are in a pile on the floor. A big wet heap that hasn't been sorted out. I pull it apart and lay it out in the same careful way my clothes were laid out for me. I kneel down next to her. The butterfly mask has slipped almost entirely off, and I put my hand between Earl's shoulder blades.

"Hey, Earl," I say. "Can you wake up?"

And just like that she shoots up, blankets and mask falling away so that she can back up against the wall. Both hands to her face to cover what I briefly see are the scars she promised me.

"Whoa, I'm not going to hurt you."

I loved Ray's scars—my love never distinguished between the accidental and the self-inflicted. I wanted to trace them, mark them. They were a way of claiming ownership over him, and because of me, he kept making them. Cut here and here and here. I would trace them when they were still bloody. Lie lazily next to him in our spot by the river and count the marks where he'd opened himself up. Ask for one more.

I want to tell Earl that I know she is a girl and that being a girl is okay. That being a girl is great, even if that's a lie.

She's just a little kid. A body that needs a bath. Small hands. Tiny feet. She has the fat belly of a little kid not grown to her full height and yet her body is already changing, subtly shifting. I got my period when I was nine. A terrifying surprise to me and a devastation to my mom.

"Oh, Emma," my mom said when she caught me pulling the stained sheets out of the dryer. I'd panicked and tried to clean them as I would have for my father's accidents, forgetting to throw in my own pajama pants. Blood and urine leave different histories.

Earl has a birthmark on her chest that looks like the state of Ohio. And then I do what I know I shouldn't and I lie. "It's okay. I've already seen your scar."

The kid doesn't say anything and continues to secure the mask either out of habit or because I'm a liar.

"You're a girl," I say gently.

"Am not."

"I see you. You're a girl and that's okay. I'm a girl too. I'm not going to hurt you."

"I'm not a girl." I hear the anger. It's an old rage. Something said before. Shouted. Whimpered. "I'm a boy, just got the wrong parts."

"Okay, Earl, what do you mean 'wrong parts'?" I ask.

"I don't have a penis. I have a *gina*." He whispers the word "gina" as if it is our secret code phrase. "My mama said God got mixed up and switched my parts with some other kid."

"So, some girl is wearing your penis around?" I ask.

Earl laughs in spite of himself. "I think it's just stuck up in, you know, there. It'll come out when it's ready."

"I'm pretty sure that's not how it works, and what's wrong with being a girl?" I ask.

"Nothing's wrong with it. I'm just not!" He's had this

conversation a hundred times before and he starts to get dressed.

"Fine. You're a boy."

"You believe me?"

"Makes no difference to me what you are. I'm used to you being a boy. It's old news."

He smiles. Grateful. My chest expands with warmth.

"Did you move him?"

"Move who?" I know exactly whom he means.

"George."

"No."

He looks surprised, and I think his surprise is like my own—he isn't accustomed to people being honest—but then he says, "He'll come for us."

I think of the empty lawn chair.

"He's dead now, I'm sure of it." The snow falls steadily. The temperature is too low for someone outside to survive the night.

"Was he dead when you left him?" Earl asks.

"No," I admit. "But he was dying and I tied him to the chair and he was just lying there on the ground."

"Lying there?"

"Yes, Jesus. He fell over in the chair. He woke up, so I tied him to the chair and then he vomited and fell over. He passed out."

Earl stares at me for a while.

"What were you doing that whole time?"

The cellar. Body brown. Skull bones visible through

skin. Like a sheet of tissue paper wrapped around a birthday present.

"You saw her," he says.

"I was with your dying father. That's plenty."

"What did he tell you?"

"Earl," I say, and reach out to grab his arm. It is a touch meant to reassure him, to hold him still so I can talk some sense into him, but he swipes at my hand and breaks free without even giving me a minute of contact. This is the same kid who let me wrap around him last night? "I'm not going to hurt you."

He says nothing.

"You don't know him. He makes me dress up like a girl. He calls me Earlene," Earl says, and then takes off his butterfly mask, and I see what else George is capable of. A face thick with scars but also fresh spots. Little red scabs over cigarette burns. A split lip.

"George did this?" I ask. "Because you are a boy?"

"I'm what he's got left. He doesn't like that."

Rage grows in me, a welcome déjà vu of a tamped-down feeling. Warm and thick and burning at the edges. I let George go, and now he's free to find Earl again.

"It's not so bad," Earl says, and the rage loses its heat, goes rigid with its sudden cooling.

I stare at his eyes now, and in that look from Earl to Emma and Emma to Earl, I feel it. The fear. George is coming; he is here in these hills.

"He didn't always want me dead. We moved here so

we could start again. He said this would fix everything. Mama said he wouldn't hurt us anymore if he was happy."

"But he did hurt you. He does. He killed your mother, didn't he."

Earl flinches a little but recovers quickly. "We moved, but he was never happy. This place wasn't what he said it would be. Maybe if it had been more like what he'd planned he would have gotten better instead of worse."

"A place doesn't just turn you, Earl."

"I don't think he meant to kill her. He just wanted to make her stop crying. He said it was all he could ever hear out here, her hollering and weeping, so he held on to her neck too long. I couldn't stop him. I should have stopped him. I tried. This place made him sick. He says we're running out of money."

"Earl," I say, his name coming out of me with such sorrow that saying anything else seems arbitrary. But then I think again and add, "Why do you want to stay here in this sad place?"

"What do you mean?" he asks. "You think it's gonna make me sick too? Make me kill someone?" His eyes are wide with fear of the possibility.

"Haven't you already killed someone? Or tried anyway?" I ask. "George. You've tried to kill your father," I say when I see he isn't getting it. How has this not occurred to him before.

"George doesn't count," he says, but I can tell he is

unsure. He isn't sure what he's capable of. I know that feeling. I've worried my whole life that I'm crazy.

"My mama's here and it isn't bad for me like it is for him. It makes me feel strong like I can make my own world, like I won't ever have to fit into anyone else's again."

"My father taught me that no one is evil by accident. You have to invite it in. Don't invite it, Earl. Leave here with me."

I reach across the distance again for Earl's small hand and he lets me take it. I lean down and keep my eyes locked on to his pupils.

"We have to hurry, Earl. We have to run."

EIGHT

When my mom walks into my hospital room her clothes flow about her in fall colors—safari tans and prairie greens and creamy stripes that make me wish I had a yogurt. A Chico's moved into the Town and Country mall near our house about a year ago and my mom started shopping there like it framed a new identity for her: "It makes me feel like I have a beach house somewhere."

Today she wears a tight tank top and an ankle-length skirt that sits too high on her waist. Her sunglasses are huge, looking to revive the '70s, and she does not take them off even when the doctor comes in to give her an update on how I've been. We do not speak to each other.

No greeting. No touching. But I can tell she wants to hug me, as if throwing her arms around me would fix anything.

During all the blocking of bleeding they had to do to save me from myself, they also found yet another something on my fallopian tube. Malignant. Another abnormal growth, but this time on my ovary and separate from the one nestled in my uterus that Ray and I had mistaken for a baby. Maybe benign. They couldn't be sure. The size of the tumor on my fallopian tube required immediate action. If they caught it now, scooped everything out, radiation might still be avoided.

During the initial diagnosis at Planned Parenthood, when I thought we were confirming a baby, they told me what I had was not a baby at all. They told me I needed to see a specialist. "It might be cancer," the young doctor whispered. In my shocked and too-young brain, I formed a question: "So we made a tumor?"

The doc looked at me quizzically and then offered ever so kindly: "It might not be malignant."

I looked "malignant" up just to see the cool, ink-to-paper definition. *Malignant: evil in nature, influence, or effect; passionately and relentlessly malevolent: aggressively malicious; tending to produce death or deterioration; tending to infiltrate, metastasize, and terminate fatally.*

Emma, accurate.

An unusual case, they assured my mom. Odd to find so big a tumor in someone so young. Both ovaries looked like possible breeding grounds for cancer, something already developing on one, the other suspiciously swollen. My mother's mother died of ovarian cancer. The doctor said an oophorectomy should cover all the dangerous possibilities in my case, a fairly simple abdominal procedure to remove both ovaries and the fallopian tube. An oophorectomy. It sounds so clumsy, so male. Ooph. The doctor told us, "We're lucky to have found it all."

Lucky.

I watched the doctor make baseball-size gestures. Big as an orange. Too risky to wait. I signed the paperwork with my mom's help. Signed away my insides. Bye-bye, Pea Baby. Good riddance to future babies. I had to sign six times to make them feel better. To ensure that a semi-healthy, eighteen-year-old woman wouldn't later decide to sue their asses. Even as my mom signed once, then twice, then three times she was crying. Big, silent tears that made her look even prettier than she already was.

Coming out of it later, I dreamed the tumor into pulpy, fruit-slice sections. The solid skin of it split open on a surgical knife blade. The blood-fruit color and texture. The taste of it on my tongue, sour. Bitter gagging. I scraped the skin clean, swallowed my insides for safekeeping. When I woke up fully, my mom was long gone. Dr. Patel was there to describe the complications they'd encountered. They'd found another cancerous lump cuddled into the lining of my uterus. They'd had to remove more than they'd originally hoped. Hysterectomy. Just a few more organs, tissues really, here and there.

Alone and dizzy and sore. The nurses wouldn't look at me or I wouldn't look at them. I had three little sessions with a hospital-hired psychologist, psychiatrist, psychopath in which I said nothing. How was I feeling? It's normal to have a sense of extreme loss. It's normal to feel some anger. Some women experience a decrease in sexual pleasure. Good, I thought. I don't want it anymore. You can have it along with my ovaries and uterus. You can keep my future orgasms in a jar.

One of the nurses or doctors saying, "Poor thing. She'll never get over this. Honey, what do you need?"

"Drugs," I answer, and she obliges. It isn't as good as cocaine, but she gets me more than I need and then, instead of blackness or sleep, there is a constant white glare. Like staring out the window at high noon after a snowstorm, like headlights bouncing off eyeballs in the middle of the night.

Today Dr. Patel is recommending radiation after all. They already spoke to me about it, but I've been playing catatonic. Besides some shameful crying when I realized how much I'd lost—gagging and boogers and crunched-up red face—I've not said a word. The nurses hate me. The doctors talk around me. It's amazing how quickly people make you into wallpaper.

I just bathed, wanting to feel clean and to examine my scar privately, but I heard my mother arrive while I was still undressed. I wish she'd stop visiting. She comes every day. Twice a day. We don't even talk to each other. She just comes and sits as if something is going to get better or change. As if Ray is going to turn out to be alive and I'm going to stop wanting to be dead. Every time I look at her I want to cry, and if I start crying, I won't stop. I hate her for this.

I rushed to put the hospital gown back on too quickly and now I feel steam trapped between my skin and the fabric. Hearing them discuss radiation treatments as if I cannot hear them, as if I am not eighteen and ready to make my own decisions, turns all that steam to liquid and it slides down toward my shoes in the form of sweat.

It's hot outside for fall. I can tell by the perspiration on my mother's upper lip and I stare out the window at the asphalt in the parking lot as they talk. It's the kind of hot that makes shimmery pools of water appear and disappear in the dips and curves of the asphalt. I stare hard, unblinking, turning the puddles into dark pools with no bottom. I fill them with pale fish and gnarled mermaids, imagine translucent hands grabbing at the lips of the pools and pulling up creatures best left in the depths.

"Emma." My mother is talking to me. Clearly she has said my name several times before I've heard it. Her eyes are pooled with unshed tears.

I blink my dry eyes and turn. The doctor whispers something that I don't catch and then shudders a little.

My mother does not see the shudder but the whisper makes her lips go thin.

"They want to do treatments."

I keep my eyes on hers so she knows I hear her. She is not asking me a question. She is stating a fact.

The doctor leaves the room. Strides out quickly. Folks here are afraid of me. It occurs to me, seeing my mother, that she is afraid of me too.

"Do you want treatments?" my mother asks.

"Will they save me?" I ask. It's my first sentence in weeks, and it comes up scratchy, possibly from disuse. They had me on a feeding tube. That was painful.

"Yes. They say that radiation should rid the rest of your body of the cells that caused the tumor. It's the best-case scenario at this point."

I look my mother in the eyes then and see her hurt. How deep it runs. How it has burned streaks of yellow into her irises and etched lines into her forehead. I see how easy it would be to fix her hurt. I could reach out and hug her or just relax my body so that she could wrap her arms around me. But I know that I am evil, that I invited it in a long time ago. And I wanted to hurt her.

"I don't want to get better," I say.

"Emma," she says. A fat tear slides down her cheek and I want to smack it away. "I need you to try."

They stripped my bed clean an hour ago so I'm sitting on the bare mattress. They launder the sheets, it seems, hourly, as if this will keep my filth from staining the hospital in some permanent way.

My feet don't touch the floor; instead, they swing little-girl loose. I'm supposed to get up and walk the room five times a day to regain my strength.

"I can have you declared mentally unfit," she says. Her voice is barely a whisper. "Considering what you did, you being eighteen now won't matter. I can make the decisions, but I'd rather you did the right thing for yourself."

"You're going to put me in the loony bin?"

"No, they don't have loony bins anymore," she says. "That's not a thing, but I will take over, Emma. I have power of attorney. You need help. I don't know when things got so bad, but I can do better as your mother now. I can fix this. Are you still—"

"Still what? Suicidal?"

"I was going to say using."

"Do you mean alcohol? Marijuana? Coke? I wasn't planning on *not* doing it, but if you mean dosing up on all three to try to unsuccessfully kill myself, I guess I'll take a break for a minute. The hospital has given me some better shit anyway."

"Jesus, Emma. When did you get so selfish?"

"Like father like daughter, I guess." It was a good call on her part. Selfish. I realized it in a flash right then. I'd imagined myself pathetic, unlucky, evil, but not what I really had become: Completely self-absorbed. Unsympathetic.

"You aren't your father," she says but I can tell she isn't sure.

"I don't want them to do more things to my body. They've done plenty and if you tell them they can now pump poison into me without my permission then . . ." I say, changing the subject.

"Then what, Emma? And since when do you care what you put in your body? Do you know how many drugs they found in your system?" she asks.

"Three," we say at the same time.

"That's right. Three different narcotics, and that's not counting the alcohol." The shake in her voice is gone. She looks momentarily angry but it drains out of her as quickly as it arrived. "What if I just tell them to keep at it? To save you whether you like it or not?"

"Well, Denise, I won't ever forgive you and you can't save someone who doesn't want to be saved." Ray always called my mom Denise. She hated it. She wanted to be his mother. I should give her more credit for that. I move my arms to cover my belly, which is sensitive to even the potential of pressure. The row of Frankenstein stitches is fresh.

"I had one baby, three miscarriages, and a dead husband before I turned thirty. You don't get to quit. You have to keep trying to be happy."

"You quit on Daddy." I didn't know about the miscarriages.

"That's not fair."

"You quit on me."

"Emma," she says, and her voice cracks in a way I haven't heard before, as if I've reached deep down into her this time. Gotten at her in a way I never have before. "After your father's accident, I wasn't right. He was good to you, but he was never good to me. We weren't good for each other, and to have him die like that before we could do right by each other, well, it was too much for me. I was too young. I should have asked for help."

In the months after Daddy died, she'd disappear for days. Go into her bedroom and climb under the covers and slip into what could have been a coma. There were days when I thought she was dead, when I had to prove to myself by holding a mirror under her nose that she was still alive.

"You thought you were pregnant, didn't you?" she asks, interrupting my thoughts. "That's why you cut yourself like that? Were you trying to abort the baby or something?"

"Something like that," I say. Explaining to her that it was the opposite, that I wanted to see the baby, hold it, prove to Ray and to myself that it was there, is impossible. The logic of it gone as soon as the drugs left my system. Before that even. When the cut started to burn, reality sliced through everything I'd ingested and shocked my system back into life. Saved my sad little life.

"If you thought you were pregnant, you must have been sexually active."

I continue to stare at her and she can see her own stubbornness in my face.

"Come on, Emma. You can talk to me about this."

"Fuck you." I pull my arms tighter around my belly, thump my feet down onto the floor so that I'm standing. I feel a bit dizzy, the room spins, but I hold my ground. I'm wearing the lousy hospital nightgown they provide once they've got you trapped. The kind with the slit up the back and the three ties that won't stay tied no matter how many knots you put in them. My gown is white with pale blue flowers, and my scabby, surgical wound glares right through the pilled-up cotton.

I hadn't planned to cut into myself. Ray had gotten ahold of enough coke to either kill us or keep us happy for months. We chose the former, fronting it with weed and chasing it with alcohol. The antidepressants I was on were an added bonus, so I shared a handful of those with Ray too. Somewhere in there with my body buzzing happily along it occurred to me that the doctors were wrong. Pea Baby was real. I could hear it inside of me purring like a kitten. I tried to tell Ray but the words wouldn't form or he wouldn't listen, or both, so I found Ray's pocket knife and opened myself up. The cut, gaping red and warm, weeping the loss of what was never there, woke me up.

"You were nine pounds one ounce when you were born," my mother is saying. "So healthy. They took you away and cleaned you up. I didn't see you for hours and when they brought you back I told them they'd brought me the wrong baby. I had a fit. You seemed too small. Too red. Your father had to calm me down."

Silence.

"Later I was so angry at myself for not recognizing you. What kind of mother doesn't know her own child? I couldn't forgive myself, and now here I am again. I don't recognize you, Emma. I haven't in years and I don't know what to do to get back to you. I'd wish it different for you from day one if I could. From the moment I found out you were growing inside of me, but I can't."

"I don't need you," I say, and even as I say it I can hear how absurd it sounds, and as if to make it less unbelievable, I add, "I wish you'd died and Daddy had lived."

Her body stiffens. I see her take three deliberate breaths before speaking.

She says, "You did a lot of damage to yourself, Emma."

"I don't remember most of it."

"I don't see how that's possible."

"Ray was my memory."

"Well, he's gone now. What's your plan?" she asks. "If it isn't to get well or forgive me for whatever heinous acts you think I've done, what will you do next?"

"I'm leaving."

"That's it? That's your big plan."

"Ray and I wanted to travel. I'll do it alone. I want to be alone."

"You wanted to travel? Well, why didn't you just do

that? Seems to me that you wanted to ruin yourselves. Ray was, at least, successful," she says, and then turns pale. "I didn't mean that."

"I'll travel and kill myself. The radiation is supposed to ensure I live, right? Well, no radiation. Just me on the road till death do us part."

Before I can think to stop her, she moves forward and yanks up the gown. Cold air rushes in. My wound flashes red.

"This, baby girl," she says, and for a minute, I think she's going to slap me with the hand that isn't holding up the hospital gown. "This cannot be run away from or fixed. You have to start again. You have to forgive yourself and make this right."

I smack her hand away.

All the fight in me has worked its way out through my pores to shimmer and slide like a fog around my mother and me.

"I loved him," I say, and she studies me. I hold her gaze and I see when she gets it. Her eyes crinkle and then her face falls. I expect disgust or rage but she just looks sad.

"You mean Ray? You and Ray? That would never have worked and you know it."

"Why couldn't it have worked?"

"Honey."

"You did not know him." My throat feels tight, the burn from the harm I've done to myself flares up like fire.

"Frank and I knew more than he thought we did."

"Don't talk about him! You didn't know him like I did. I did. *I* knew him." I pound my fist to my breastbone as hard as my tired body will let me.

She sits next to me on the bed, defeated. Our arms touch.

"I need to leave, Mom. I need to get out of here. It's not your fault or maybe it is, but it's probably just my fault. I don't know how to be normal or happy or sober."

We sit quietly. She leans against me.

"Ray always wanted to see the Badlands," I say. "I'll stop using. I'll go there and it will help me figure out what I need to do next."

"I think you should stay," my mother says. "Get help."

"I know."

She rises from the bed and I can tell she wants to say something else. Maybe *I love you* or *I won't let you go*, but she says nothing.

A nurse comes in to take my mother's place. They pass each other in the doorway as if they haven't even seen each other.

I can feel where my mother's arm sat in contact with mine. Her touch sits with me while the nurse takes my vitals.

"You need rest," she says. "The wound won't heal and you'll have those stitches a lot longer."

"I don't mind," I say, breaking my rule to never speak to any of them. I haven't seen her before but she still looks surprised to hear my voice. Someone has told her about the crazy girl in 801 who tried to abort her own cancer as if a tumor and a fetus are the same damn thing. *Didn't her brother die too?* they'd all whisper. *Did she kill him? Maybe he tried to kill her?* I saw them gossiping about it, whispering outside my door and shivering as if I'm not just tragic but also dangerous. A serial killer already made.

"What an odd thing to say. You don't mind?"

I don't answer.

Ray and I were always touching when we were alone. Our backs pressed to each other as we faced away from each other on the bed. Our arms linked as we shared headphones. We considered ourselves one body, one pile. The warmth of him near me like a child's blanket or a teddy bear. He loved me.

"Don't cry," the nurse says. "Jesus. You're crying. Stop it now." The nurse pats me too harshly on the back, as if she's confused about whether she is burping me or comforting me. "I'll get you something."

She disappears briefly and returns to press two pills into my palm. I tell myself that at least it's not alcohol or weed or cocaine. It's not the same using I've done before.

I pull it together and stop crying, mostly to make the nurse feel better.

"You want me to see if I can catch your mother for you?"

I shake my head and lie back on my pillow.

"I'll get your bed made up again for you and I'll get you something else to help you sleep."

I curl up on the bare bed. I pull pieces of Ray into my mind. I've been practicing. Teaching myself how to bring him back.

I begin with his smell. All of it. The sweetness of him and the sweat. Then I remember how he felt against me. His hair on my neck. His hands wrapped around me to rest on my belly. He hooks one thumb into the waistline of my jeans. Then I animate him. Feel his chest rise, his breath on my neck. I scrunch my eyes tighter and feel him twine his legs through mine. I work harder still and reach back with my hand to feel the rip in his jeans. I reach through and touch his soft thigh. His body. My body. We are the same.

"I love you, Gobs."

He lifts his head to whisper into my ear, his breath tickling like feathers. "Rest now, Emma. I'm here."

I let myself drift.

NINE

The snow is deeper than it looks. My boots sink in high enough to catch its chill. The sun ricochets off the white ground.

"The barn's not far," Earl says over his shoulder. "It's where I stay most of the time, and it's where George keeps the truck and all the winter supplies."

Earl tied on his butterfly mask again before we left the diner. When he turns to speak to me, the sunlight bounces off its crinkles and folds, making him look like he's caught fire.

"You don't have to keep your mask on," I say. "I've seen what's underneath. It doesn't bother me."

"It's for safety," he says, and I don't ask or argue. I

know what it feels like to want to hide. Such scars are evidence of a very private emptying of the soul.

Earl stops. I run right into him and fall backward in the snow.

I wrestle myself up, brushing snow from my butt. My hands hum with cold, but they aren't shaking. I have not thought about Vicodin in some time.

"Where'd your scar come from?" he asks.

"I was sick. Before I went on the run. I told you that, didn't I?"

"Sick how? The flu?"

I almost say yes, just so he can believe this simple thing.

"No, no. Cancer. I had a hysterectomy."

"What's it mean?"

"They took out my uterus and ovaries," I say. *This might help her depression as well*, the doctor told no one in particular before I slipped under.

"What does that mean?"

"I can't have babies," I say, as if it is a simple fact like *I can't roll my tongue* or *My left foot is bigger than my right*. The permanence of the fact that my body has been emptied out, however, never fails to make me feel like there is a dark, empty spot in me. A hollow place. All my remaining organs shrinking back from that dark, empty spot, nothing moving in to warm or replace what was or might have been.

"Is that bad?"

"Let's just keep walking," I say. The world around us is monotone and bleak. Its harshness is working its way through the layers of my clothes and into the already deep cracks in my lips, grooving them deeper. I've hung on to George's ski mask, and I know I should put it on. I can't bring myself to do it. Instead, I trade it from hand to hand so that I can wrap the knit around each fist for warmth.

"There's good stuff in my barn," Earl says, not noticing my tone. I'm grateful for the interruption to my thoughts. "George always brought the most back before the snows. Extra clothes. Tons and tons of food. This storm is too early so we aren't ready, but he did just make a regular run. We can use the gas for your car. We might not even need what's in the truck."

"She's a van, not a car. And you should call her Veronica," I say. Earl giggles. He sounds like a little boy, looks like a little boy even now after I've seen what body he was born into.

"George said we were done here. He brought back more gas than usual. Gonna burn it down for the assurance."

"Insurance."

"I said insurance."

"I thought we had to siphon gas from the truck?"

"I didn't say that word."

"'Siphon'? No, but it means get gas out of the truck. You need to stop lying to me."

“I wasn’t lying.”

“Well, we’re on the same team now so tell me the full truth.”

What a hypocrite I am. *Tell me the full truth*, I say to him as if I’ve ever done that or even ever thought it to be the right thing. What would I say to him that would be truthful? *I found your mother rotting in the cellar next to the cans of gas I need to get out of here. Want to step over her body and help me grab a couple?* Truth is not kind or necessary.

“We are on a team?” he asks. “The Emma and Earl team?”

“Why not?” I stumble and catch myself with my hands. My fingers dig into the snow. I’d pay big money for gloves right now, but all I have are my sleeves and George’s old ski mask. I pull one sleeve down over my frozen fingers and wrap the hat more purposefully over the other hand. I deserve the discomfort even as it turns into pain. “Are there full gas cans in the barn?” I ask, willing myself to stop thinking so much.

“Yes.”

“Fantastic. We can carry them back to Veronica and head out. It gets dark early around here.”

“Super early. And I’m not leaving. This is my home.”

“I can’t leave you here. Same team. Remember? You’ll come with me and then you can come back later if you want.” I say this but lies are buried too shallowly. Surely if I get him to the cops, if they see this place, the bodies, the decay, Earl will never see it again.

"You'd really take me with you?" Earl asks. "You'd keep me if I went with you?" The sweet hesitance in his voice makes me feel teary. He is braced for rejection.

"I'll get you to a safer place. I can promise that." I feel a twinge. I'm lying. When have I ever been safe?

"No place is safer. This is the only place I make sense."

There is truth in what he says, but telling himself this is also not the right truth to share so I change the subject and ask, "So why didn't George burn the place down?"

"He didn't get around to a lot of things."

"He's a real prize."

Earl misses the sarcasm. "He isn't. He said he'd burn me up with the ghost buildings if I wasn't better, and I love this place. I want to keep it."

"Jesus," I whisper. I stand still in the snow, but Earl keeps moving, not noticing that I've stopped. It's painful to stop. The cold air settles on my exposed skin, fits itself to my pores. I stay still for as long as I can to watch Earl. A boy—no more than eight—smart enough to survive on his own. His long legs in their rain boots stretch up from the snow. He is all sinew and strength and defiance.

The daylight is changing around us, moving into afternoon in a way that makes the night already feel too close. The days are short here. Time is fleeting. I will my feet to move and catch up with Earl.

"I did it on purpose," he says quietly. I wonder if he said it once already and I didn't hear because he says it again: "I did it on purpose. On purpose."

"What *it,* Earl?"

"Killed him. Tried to do him dead. And I don't feel bad about it. Not a bit," Earl says. "Dying might not be so bad."

"Most people fight it pretty hard."

"I'd be super quiet. Like the woods right now. Like this but warm. Maybe even with snow, but the snow would be a blanket. Something I could get underneath of. I like that."

"Death is not warm or cold or anything. It's just done," I say.

"But I could be done here. On my land."

"You mean if George burned you up for the *assurance*? Earl, you're eight. You'll live a long time if you stop being so gruesome. Plus, George is surely dead by now. You'll have to find someone else to burn you up."

We've reached the barn door. Earl begins to push, to put his full weight into it, and only moves it enough to dig it in deeper to the snow.

With the promise of shelter from the wind, I feel even colder. Impatient.

Earl doesn't answer but his head tilts to the sky. Above us is a door that must lead to the hayloft.

"How we gettin' up there?" I ask.

Earl looks at me like I'm stupid: "Climb."

"Dermit," I mumble. Earl smiles.

Pine trees hug the barn. Three cluster to the right of the barn door itself and lead up to the loft like some kind of legless ladder. The long trunks actually become quite plentiful in terms of branches as soon as they hit the second story of the barn but, until then, they are noble stalks of trees that I can't imagine finding a way to hold on to.

"Are we supposed to shimmy up those?"

"Yeah. I do it all the time. You've got an advantage 'cause the snow gives you a leg up."

"Uh-huh," I say.

"You go first."

"Why?"

"That way I can help," Earl says, and laces his fingers together, as if I'm going to put my foot in his hands.

"My boobs weigh more than you," I say, and he giggles. His laugh warms me. "Fine, I'll give it a go."

I tuck the ski mask into my jacket pocket and stand at the base of the three trees and rub my hands together. There are nubs here and there, spots where branches have broken off. A real climber would go for it, finding the tiny notches and bulbs to get to the top.

"I can tell you where to put your feet," Earl says. It's a kind offer since I'm still rubbing my hands together while wondering how to get out of this. "It's easy." He points to a knob on the left tree as he taps my left foot with his hand and another knob on the tree to the right for my right foot. "You just use these two trees until you get to the branches and then you just fit your left foot in the crack of the door and you're in."

"I hear an overuse of the word 'just' coming out of you," I say.

"What?"

"Nothing. Here I go."

I fall before I even have both hands and feet on the tree. Luckily, the snow is forgiving.

"Here I go," I say.

"You already said that."

I roll my eyes at him and then there's his laugh. So young and so pleased with me. I smack my hands together and try again, shimmying up between two of the three trees like it's something I've done before, and I feel a strange pride in myself, in this girl showing off for little Earl.

Once I hit branches, it's no problem and I make my way to door level, stretching my left leg out to slide onto the ledge of the barn door. Earl is clapping as I reach out and grab the frame with my hand and make the hop inside.

I'm in the hayloft and Earl is already at the top of the tree, pulling himself inside. There is a drop-off ahead of me but the loft stretches halfway across the barn. To my right is a pile of blankets and some thick candles that have melted into the boards.

"In the summer, I live up here. In the winter, I stay downstairs so I can be close to the stove."

"It's freezing in here."

"George put in a wood burner. Keeps it toasty." He points to an old pipe stretching up through the eaves and piercing a hole through the ceiling.

"There's wood in the stove downstairs. I'll get it going for us. Come down with me."

We climb the old ladder to the first floor of the barn; the rungs creak under my boots but hold steady.

"We aren't staying long," I say. "Don't put too much effort into making it warm."

Earl works on the fire and I inspect the rest of the barn. In the farthest, darkest corner is the supposed truck all covered over with a canvas. It looks smaller than a truck should, and I know it is going to disappoint in some way that I can't yet determine so I leave it.

Instead, I discover boxes of canned goods, blankets, and several full gas cans. Hanging on one wall are snowshoes and ski poles. I can't stop smiling.

Earl has flames already eating at the wood and twigs in the stove's belly and I join him near a small wooden table with one chair. The table is covered with his tiny objects. Just like the ones I saw in the woods. There's a small stockpile of tinfoil, a jar of what looks like silver paint, child safety scissors, a bottle of Elmer's glue, and a few other odds and ends. There are sheets of tinfoil that have been flattened out and then folded evenly into squares for safekeeping. Next to these are hundreds of his tinfoil cutouts. They shine in the meager light coming from the stove. There's also a whole zoo of animals, and the creatures are all proportionate to each other. The rhinoceros with wide circular feet is small enough to fit in my palm but big enough so that the tiniest of the birds can sit between his shoulder blades.

"It's my mayonaisery," Earl says proudly.

"Your what?" I ask. Then I think, *menagerie.*

"I was doing wood carving for a long time, but George took my knife away after I stabbed him that one time, so then I started using diner supplies."

"Good for you," I say. "For the stabbing *and* the use of diner supplies." There are trees made of yellow and red twist ties that I recognize as the same type of sky-high pine trees we just climbed. He's also imitated thick maples, skinny dogwoods, and the sweep of a weeping willow.

"Mom is an artist too. She can paint." He disappears into the shadows of a far corner, coming back with a small framed painting in his hands—five by seven at the largest. "It's me," he says. I take it from him and stare at the sweet little face. He's younger. Four, maybe five, and his face is free of scars.

"This is how she saw you," I say, knowing that this is

a portrait of a little boy. Not a girl. Not something confused or in between.

"She called me Little Man," he says, and I can feel that I'm going to cry. I rub at my eyes quickly and hand him back the painting.

"I'll call you Little Wing. It's what my father called me."

"Do you want to see what they can do?" Earl asks.

"Of course."

Earl moves to the other side of the table where the shadows are thicker. His hands disappear down and his face becomes focused. Then he raises his hands up above his head.

I'm watching his face so closely that I almost miss what he's trying to show me. It's the glint of them that makes me shift my head. On the tabletop, his menagerie is moving. At first, it looks like it could be a trick of the light. A shift of flames in the stove making the tiny animals look as if they are animated, but then my brain adjusts again. The animals are moving. He has them on fishing line attached to his fingers. Their bodies stepping forward. A horse rears up on its hind legs. A rabbit takes one hop.

A small bird tests the air with his wings and tilts his head up to look at me, so I hold out my hand, forefinger extended and it lands there, tinfoil talons on my knuckle. Its weight is barely there. I could crush it. Clap my other hand on top of it and snuff it out. Some old piece of me wants to do it. I hear what I would have said to Ray: *If you don't do it, someone else will.*

I do not crush it. Its tiny talons adjust themselves on my finger, it shakes out its wings, puffs up, and nestles its beak into its feathers. And then, as I watch, the life in it fades and it drops off my finger, hits the table, and stays there. A lump of foil.

"How did you do that?" I ask.

"It's what I do," Earl says. He is proud, puffed up like that little bird.

"Do it again," I say, and then add, "The bird. Just the bird this time."

The little bird hops up off the floor and, wings spread, flies up into the air. It glides past my face, flaps its wings. Lands on the tabletop, pecks at the wood softly and then tilts its head up toward me.

"It's beautiful," I say. I watch the life go out of it again. A gentle leaving that takes with it not just the possible motion of the object, but also a glow that seems to originate from its center. A tiny heartbeat so subtle that perhaps I've made it up.

"I like making them. And I like doing it for you."

"It's incredible, Earl."

He looks so pleased with himself that I feel the ache of his joy deep in my heart. Something in me activated. Electric.

"Do you want to know my dream for this place?" he asks.

"Sure."

"I want to turn the ghost town part into a place to hang pictures and show off my carvings and stuff."

"A gallery?"

"Yes, like that! And artists can come live here. People who don't have any other place to be. They can make things and stay as long as they want."

"An artists' colony."

"What's that?"

"It's what you're describing. Places set up to promote art. My stepbrother wanted to go to one, but they don't take people under eighteen."

"A colony," he says with awe. "So I didn't make it up?"

"It's a thing."

"I want people like you and me to come and stay and make things so they feel more better about themselves."

"That's a beautiful idea, Earl." It is. It makes me wish I was younger, more hopeful.

"You sound sad," he says. He's right of course. I sound sad because I am sad.

"I just think this place isn't what you think it is. It's sad here. Dangerous. You could get out of here. Go to school. Find what you're talking about somewhere else." My voice goes up at the end as if I'm asking him a question. It's reassuring to neither of us.

"I don't think so."

"I do. Didn't George bring you out here because he

thought it was going to fix things? And didn't it make everything worse?"

Earl nods yes to this and then pauses. "You think I could find a place like that without making it myself?"

"I do."

"If I did come with you, could I bring a few of them with me? And Mom's painting? That too?" he asks.

"Of course!"

"There are blankets upstairs. I'll go get them, and I'll bring down those candles too."

Earl's headed up the ladder and I breathe deeply. I feel the weight of what I've promised him. I can't raise him. I know nowhere to take him besides the hospital. If the story plays in his favor, he'll end up in foster care. If it doesn't, he'll end up in juvenile detention. What other options are there? Emma and Earl drive off into the sunset? I could hold his hand while we both jump off the edge of the Badlands. I stand in the dimly lit barn and let the sick feeling ripple through me for a moment before I peer out the cracks in the large barn door. The snow is deep. The light continues to wane. Leaving him here can't be the best choice. A body in motion must stay in motion.

I sink to the ground. My back is to the door. My pants are wet from falling in the snow. I should rise and stand by the fire but I'm tired. So tired. I look around the little room at all Earl's creations. They're treasures.

"Look out below!" He drops a blanket, an unlit candle, and another blanket.

I rest where I am a moment longer, tilt my head back and look up at the cracks in the loft floor where light streams down through air faint with dust. I see Earl moving up there. Flitting around happy, and I feel his joy in my chest. It feels good. Hushed. Warm. Soft. It's that toe-curling, something-great-about-to-happen feeling. *Maybe this is just what it feels like to want to be alive. To have a plan. A next step. A sustainable desire.*

But then a new sensation comes. This one concrete and identifiable. A thump. A push. I feel it against my back and then harder a third time, up by my head. Something is pushing at the barn door and then banging and banging again. Thudding right at the spot where my body rests as if the whole of the barn door can be hit hard enough to give way. Something or someone is trying to get in.

TEN

"Emma," Ray whispers as he plops down at the breakfast table. "Do you ever feel it coming on in your finger bones?"

My face flushes red. Lately it does that a lot. Often around Ray. I can't tell if he really doesn't notice or if he's just pretending not to notice. I'm sixteen going on seventeen—Ray is already eighteen—and it's silly, but I feel different, like something is actually going to change this year on the arbitrary day of my birth.

He reaches over and pinches me, which only makes me flush a deeper red.

"It feels like something great is about to happen?" He's got a box of cereal in his hand. It's the blue box of sugary flakes he hides in his room so Denise doesn't throw it out. He pulls two bowls from the cupboard, pouring mine first because that's the kind of guy he is.

"You trying out new meds or something," I growl.

"That's not kind," he says, and I hear that I've deflated him. Hit home in the way only I can. I don't like it when Ray is happy outside of me. It's like I don't even know him anymore. He becomes this other thing, separate from my life, and I have the urge to crush this happy new thing called Ray. It's unkind, I know, but it rises up so strong these days. I've almost given up trying to stop it.

"I didn't get enough sleep and I don't know what you are talking about."

"Well, I feel good. You should join me."

I study his face for his crazy. It's there. It's always there, and while it's true that his triumphant grin looks a bit maniacal, he looks otherwise pure in his happiness. Ready to take on some aspect of the world that I think we should hide from.

"I had this dream last night. Want to hear it? It was a revelation."

"What is this? Bible school?"

"They call it Sunday school, you heathen, and stop ruining it. Just listen. I dreamed we were standing on the edge of a canyon."

"That's it?"

"Yes, it was you and me. The thing was that we were surrounded by red rocks, shifting and moving as if they were the vertebrae of some great big monster. New canyons kept forming all the time. Our toes hanging right over the edge but we weren't scared. *You*, you were happy."

Ray smiles broadly at me and my heart aches. The joy on his face is contagious, but I do my best to fight it off. He's been lying to me lately, thinking I won't notice.

"Jesus, Ray. Are you some kind of greeting card now?" I slam my notebook shut. I've taken to drawing with black ink. Digging lines into the white paper over and over until they tear through. My mother found it and threatened a therapist.

"Shut up," Ray says. "I won't let you ruin this. It was an amazing dream. So, suddenly these green mountains start popping up in the distance or maybe they were always there and a path starts to snake from us into the hills. The path is all furry and green. It looks like moss." He stops talking and grins at me, satisfied. He is not wearing mascara this morning. He always wears mascara, and he has a purple bruise on his neck.

"Is that a hickey?" I ask.

"What? Where?"

"On your neck. Is it a hickey?"

"Of course not. Where would I get a hickey?"

He's lying. Flat-out lying.

"So that's your dream? Some canyony shit?"

"I guess I'm not describing it right."

"Where were you last night?" I ask. At midnight, he

sneaked out of the house. He got up off the couch where we fell asleep watching B movies, put on his sneakers, rubbed water through his hair, and left. I could smell deodorant on him—pine scented. He climbed out the basement window. It wasn't the first time he'd done it, but it was the first time I'd stayed awake long enough to actually watch him go. I followed his movements with my eyes, daring him to look and notice that I was awake. He never looked at me. Not even a glance over his shoulder as he climbed out the basement window.

"We weren't scared," he says, shrugging off my question without even the decency to look surprised. "And you weren't going to jump because you wanted to die. And it wasn't our dumb pact. You were going to fly until you found ground and then walk the path."

"Now I know this is Sunday school, and since when was our pact dumb?"

"You're not listening."

Ray's face shifts. His usual sadness creeps in. I should feel victorious. This was what I wanted, right?

"Where were you last night?" I ask again.

"Out."

"We tell each other everything, don't we?"

"Always and forever. Gobs loves Emma and Emma loves Gobs." He holds out his pinkie finger to do our ironic pinkie promise, the one we've been doing since way before we decided to make it ironic.

"I don't trust him," I say, experimenting. I didn't follow Ray, but I have a guess as to where he went. I want to give him a chance to tell me what has changed with him.

"Him who?"

"What does he want from you?"

"Nothing."

"You always tell me."

"I always tell you what?"

"What's going on. We tell each other everything."

"I just tried to tell you something. You didn't listen."

"You mean the dream you had in which I jump to my death?"

"Emma!" He slams his fist into the breakfast table and his cereal bowl jumps. Milk and softened flakes splash out.

"I'm sorry," I say, but I am not sorry. I'm angry and lately I can't get away from the anger. When it crops up, I dive into it. Let it hold on to me. I go deeper.

"It was about us figuring out how to be happy. We were there. In the Badlands. We walked out into the beginning and the end of the world. The sky was huge above us. Starless but I knew they were coming, the stars. Like we just had to put them up there. One at a time."

"Ray?"

"What?"

"Why do you keep sneaking out?"

"I can't sleep. I go over to play poker. Everybody goes. It's not a big deal."

"Since when do you go where everybody goes?"

"Not today, Emma. Please. Just let it be for today."

"Are you getting high with him?" I ask. He doesn't answer. "Fine," I say. I give him a peck on the cheek when I stand up from the table, and he reaches around to grab me. He shifts in his chair and presses his face to my belly. I let my hands hang loose, refusing to hug him back, but then I fold and put my arms awkwardly around his head. I look down at his dark hair; its purposeful disarray is charming. The pale skin of his part almost blue.

"I love you," he says.

"I know you're lying to me. I don't understand why."

"I'm sorry."

"Don't be sorry, just don't lie to me. It scares me."

"Okay."

"Okay, what?"

"I can't today, Emma. J-just," he stutters, "just know that things change. It's normal."

I walk away angry. Break free of him and lock myself in my bedroom.

I press my back to the door and look around. The pink walls are not my fault (the last owners had a much girlier little girl), but the white desk and the Guns N' Roses poster are mine. There is a plethora of Hello Kitty junk on my dresser. The lamp is a wagon wheel—one of the only items I kept from the last house I lived in, when my father was still alive. The room is a collection of odd past interests that no longer equal me. It is lonely, this stale room. I want out immediately, but I am too stubborn to leave and admit that change is normal.

I sink to the floor. Wait for the moment to pass.

I wake up in the night and Ray is already gone. The basement that we've dubbed ours is empty. We ate too many Oreos and watched MTV and read aloud to each other. We do this on Sundays. Hole up together and refuse to surface.

He's restarted the VCR so that the movie we were watching together when I fell asleep is playing from the beginning again.

I slip on my jeans, my shoes. I climb the stairs. They creak under me but my stepfather's snores are louder.

It's raining outside. Nothing heavy but enough that the walk will soak me. Ray's Schwinn is gone from its usual tilt against the garage. He's taken to it lately, riding it with his black jeans tucked into his Converses. His long-sleeve shirts flash with safety pins while his wallet chain clanks against the red crossbar. He used to refuse to ride it. Frank bought it for him a year ago when he took away Ray's driver's license. He rode it exactly once, because his father insisted he try it out, a humiliating experience. Ray rode it up and down the driveway as if he were a six-year-old trying out his big-boy bike. After that he parked it, not touching it until a month ago, when the midnight rides started.

My '69 Mustang coupe is parked at the end of the drive. I bought it for $650 off an old man who was the original owner. My father would have been proud of me. The engine needs to be replaced, it's underpowered, but I haven't had time to figure out how to get a new one for free yet so the old one stays.

I put the car in neutral and roll it down the road a bit before turning the key in the ignition.

We live in the more expensive part of town now, and have for the past four years. Frank is a comptroller, whatever that is. It's the longest I've ever lived in one place. Dad moved us from apartment to apartment. Each one shittier than the last. I miss being nomadic. I don't trust our big house in our white suburb with its vigilant police force. They are good at paying attention to anyone who doesn't fit. If I'm caught out here tonight, driving around, they will bring me straight home, make me ring my own doorbell to wake my parents. I don't care. It's worth the risk, because if this happens, Ray's absence will be discovered and we'll both be housebound.

I drive past community green space and the row of frat houses that signal the university has begun. The city of Dayton looms ahead. The sidewalks lose their brick and the street signs turn basic, more informational than ornate.

We all call him Coach Matt even though he is more a science teacher than a coach. He is barely twenty-two and got hired straight out of college to fill in for Mrs. Weir the Science Queer, who had a nervous breakdown mid-year. Coach Matt is somehow related to the superintendent, which surely got him the job. He coaches girls' soccer and dabbles in chemistry. He is quite the opposite of Mrs. WQ. He is young and energetic. The girls love him. He's cute enough in a suntanned, athletic kind of way. It's rumored he falls asleep in faculty meetings and doesn't believe in underwear. He hosts late-night poker games in his house downtown and students sometimes attend.

I don't like Coach Matt. I'm the only one who doesn't. Ray and I watched for a while, as we are prone to do. We watched the girls giggle and fall all over each other when he walked by. We watched relationships split as Coach Matt supposedly showed favor to one silly high school girl over another. We wagered he'd sleep with Emily first—a blonde with perky tits and most likely to never tell—and then work his way through the rest of the senior class, hitting all the eighteen-year-olds before he had to consider anyone underage. The year would be over before it became illegal.

I park outside Coach Matt's house. I feel anxious. More anxious than I should.

Ray joined the poker game about a month ago, right around the time he stopped wanting to gossip about who was who and whether or not Coach Matt was a pedophile or just a lucky dude.

He'd asked Ray to stay after class one day. I waited

outside that room for fifteen minutes for Ray that day—late to my next class without an excuse—and all Ray would say when he came out was: "He's cool."

Ray learned to play poker. Tried to teach me but I told him it was stupid. Then he started disappearing at night and one of the football players at school was saying hey to him in the hallway.

Coach Matt's house is in South Park. An area folks say is up-and-coming. We almost lived here once. My dad wanted to rent an old Victorian, but it fell through when he couldn't make the security deposit.

Coach Matt's house is an old bungalow with Brazilian flags out front. The front porch is littered with running shoes and soccer cleats, hiking boots and discarded Gatorade bottles. It wasn't hard to figure out which was his.

My car door creaks open and I shut it gently behind me before I climb the porch stairs. Music is playing inside. Something too loud and mainstream. Ray would never listen to it.

I creep in. Shut the front door behind me.

I expect to hear laughter. The smell of cigars. I am an intruder, but Coach Matt's house is infamous. Everyone coming and going with ease. I've not been here before, but it doesn't seem like I'm doing anything wrong, not until I round the corner. I see them both at the same time.

Ray's shirt is off. His hands on the small of Coach

Matt's back. Their faces pressed together. No space between their bodies.

They are one thing.

I stand there too long. Not because I want to watch—I don't—but because I can't understand what I'm seeing. Their bodies seem so urgent. No one else here. No poker game, and they look like they've done this before. They know each other. It is not how Ray has ever touched me and I see how much of our life together I've made up in my head.

"Emma?" Ray asks. Truly shocked. "What the fuck?"

"Is that your sister?"

"Get out!" Ray has never been this angry with me before.

"Don't yell at her, man," Coach Matt says.

"Fuck you!" I turn and run out onto the porch.

I pause under this man's roof. Heart pounding. I count to ten, slowly. If Ray loves me, he will come out the front door.

He doesn't come.

I hop in my car and drive through the city. I drive to the river where Ray and I like to go. It's a dirty river, low in most seasons, but it runs through the city and once flooded so high that it left its mark on the buildings downtown. Our spot is at a bend in the river where an old concrete bench sits sadly crumbling. There are also a few trees here that throw shade when the sun is at its highest. For now it is dark and I settle myself out in the open so I can stare up at the sky.

I shut my eyes. I wish I were the type to cry.

When I wake, the sky is clear. Ray is next to me.

"He's your teacher," I say.

"I know."

"It's not right."

"I know."

"What does it mean?"

"It means I'm in love."

"It can't mean that."

"Why can't it?" he asks, but he's not really looking for me to answer. "You know when I first met you, Emma, you laughed a lot. You weren't afraid. At fourteen you knew how to take apart a car and then put it back together! What girl knows how to do that?" he says, then pauses as if this is when he expects an answer. "You had a brightness in you, Emma, that made me feel like there were no rules. But lately . . ."

"Lately what?" I challenge and it comes out angry, a little spit sparking from my lips.

Ray sighs. "You're mean. The old Emma cared if I was happy. It made her happy to see me happy."

"She wasn't real."

We rest together quietly, long enough for me to wish

that I could stop being angry just for a minute. Who would I be if I could just let things go?

"Look at the sky, Emma."

I look up. The clouds are thick.

"Now shut your eyes."

I do as he says.

My back is wet. My body cold. The night is slipping into morning. The world is still quiet.

"Open," he says, and I do. Above us the sky shines. Stars twinkle down. The clouds are all but gone. "I threw them up there for you. I made it brand-new. Do you like it?" he asks.

"I do," I say, but it's the game I like and the fact that he still wants to play it with me.

"I love you, Gobby Gobs."

"I love you, Emma My Emma."

"No, I mean I really love you."

"I know."

We watch the sky together.

"Don't leave me," I say.

"I couldn't if I wanted to," he says back, and in this simple statement, I hear that he could leave me, and will if I don't stop him.

ELEVEN

My heart is pounding against my rib cage. Earl has stopped moving. *Good boy*, I think. *Stay quiet. Be still.*

"It's me, George. I'm coming in." George hisses through the cracks in the barn. "Coming in, in, in."

There is a slam of skull to wood, and then a harsh series of finger pecks, as if he is trying to hammer through with one fingernail. His shadow blocks the light as he fumbles in the snow, moving back and forth, looking for a chink in the splintered skin of the barn.

I want to run. Move. Hit. Scream. But I don't. I stand still and breathe through my nose. Short animal breaths. Terror. That's what this is. We're prey. My life has not been precious for a long time but my head is tilting up, and I'm thinking, *Hurt him and I'll kill you.*

"Bitches!" He screams the one word into the sky. The sound of it going up, up, up. It will come back down and land with an explosion.

A few straws of hay drift down from the loft above, evidence of Earl's noiseless shifting.

"I can see the smoke from the stove, you idiots. I know you're in there."

I move onto my toes, spin around in my position, and inch to the right so I can see through a crack. George is out there, red-faced and underdressed. His hair sticks up in clots as he considers the three trees from a distance and then walks over to them. He moves like Frankenstein's monster, his feet too heavy for the snow, and his left arm dark with blood that drips into the snow. Bright and red.

"Leave us alone!" I shout.

He stops. Stands perfectly still.

"I need my kid." He does not turn to my voice when he speaks.

I move away from the barn door and begin to fill a backpack that Earl's left out. I put in a couple cans of food, a sweater. I leave the bag at the foot of the ladder and go back for two gas cans. They are heavy, full enough to get Veronica to safety, and I set them next to the backpack.

When I find a new view of him, I see that he has

moved in order to put both hands to the barn door. He is trying to locate me.

"It's cold out here," he says, pressing his forehead to the barn. "Let me in so I can warm up."

Earl is above me, shaking. His body pressed to the floor. I want to reach up and reassure him, but he is too far away for touch.

"You need to leave me alone. You and your weird kid can go to hell."

"The kid is in there with you," George says. "I can smell the little shit."

"I don't have your fucking kid."

George moves sideways, closer to my voice, testing cracks in the door to see if he's found me yet. His body lands darkly on the crack I am using. He pushes his lips up against the wood and speaks.

"I can't feel my feet."

"You know where to get shelter. This isn't the only space."

"You let me in and we'll see if we can get along."

"I couldn't let you in if I wanted to," I say. It's a mistake. I've given his frozen brain what it needs to start puzzling through how I got in. He moves his face off the wood of the barn, the shadow of him staying still for the moment. He shifts his gaze to his right to re-examine the three trees.

Earl sneezes, a distinct sound, childlike and clear.

I move then, fast as I can, to the ladder. I climb the rungs and am at Earl's side, helping him to his feet.

"Shhhh," I say, and hold him to me. "Go to ground level," I say into his ear. "Uncover the truck. We may need to drive it out of here stat."

Earl does as I've told him, shaking so badly I'm afraid he won't find the first rung of the ladder, but he does and soon he is on the ground. I walk to the ledge and look down. The trees we climbed to get into the loft are within arm's reach. George is trying to climb them, so I reach out and rest my palm on the bark of one of them, give it a push. Its trunk is strong, but George notices the shift and looks up. He can't climb them. Not in his current state. His legs move as if they are made of lead and his left arm is not of much use. Drops of red hit the snow at his feet.

"Looks like climbing isn't gonna work for you today," I say.

"Well, hello there," he says, and shades his eyes with his right hand, trying to make his left look more normal by tucking it in his jeans pocket, though he winces as he does this. "You don't know what you're doing out here, do you, pretty girl?"

For a moment, his words cut through me. The familiar nausea of not knowing what I'm doing returns. If I trace back the origins of what brought me to this moment, standing high above a monster of a man, I will find only my own evil heart. I wasn't born with it. It came later, my desire to direct and control. Ray was like one of Earl's tinfoil creations.

"I'm going to leave this place and I'm taking Earl with me. I know that much. I also know there is no way you are going to be able to climb those trees."

"Earl," he scoffs. "Earl isn't real and neither am I and neither are you. This place made us all up and it'll take us all down."

"Don't put your crazy on me, mister."

He stares up at me blankly for a time and then a smile spreads across his face.

"I wasn't always this crazy. Don't get me wrong, I've always been on the mean side, but this place. The solitude of it. Well, it changes you."

"You killed your wife. That indicates long-term crazy to me."

"Fair enough, but I do prefer to think of it as putting her out of her misery. I'll do you the same favor if you'd like."

"I'm good."

"Hey. New subject. Wanna know how I hurt my arm?" he asks.

"Not really," I say, and turn toward the ladder. If the truck has keys, maybe, just maybe we can get it started, bust through the wooden door, and run right over George on our way out.

"There's a man out here in these woods. Says he knows

you. He got me in the biceps a few times with a switchblade before I could get the cellar door to shut on him."

I stop in my tracks and turn back toward George's voice.

"Lowell Smith is his name. Says people call him Smitty."

"I don't believe you," I say.

I've come to the edge of the loft again. I can see George down below. His body big and filthy even from this height.

"Here's proof if you need it," George says, and throws a shiny object up into the loft. It plops down between my boots. I lean over to pick it up, feel the weight of it in my hand before I am ready to admit that it is Lowell's switchblade. The one I left him so his chances of survival might not be a total joke.

"That's not possible."

"Because you tried to kill him? Well, he wasn't as hurt as he looked, and these woods aren't as mysterious as they seem if you know the right paths. I've helped him along a bit. And don't worry, he won't get you unless I say so. Got him locked up safe and sound with all our monsters." He grins up at me widely.

"He's nothing to me," I say, and slip the switchblade into my jacket pocket.

"Maybe. Or maybe you care a little. Maybe you don't want to be a murderer after all. You shot him. Left him to die. Sweetheart, if you think about it, I actually saved him. Even after he stabbed me I still had his best interests at heart. He's pretty pathetic really. He keeps telling me he has a kid. Over and over like I give a fuck," he says. "My God, think about this! If he dies out here, it's not my fault. I haven't hurt him. *You did* and *you* could still save him. Right your wrong and all that shit. I'll tell you what. Give me my kid and I'll give you your dumb-fuck boyfriend."

"You gave up your right to Earl the first time you hurt him."

George is momentarily enraged. A new look on his horrible face. Flashing across with such force that I know he is still too strong for me. Adrenaline, testosterone, hate, whatever it is that makes him run will overcome frostbite and stab wounds in order to get through me to Earl. Then he tilts his face to the ground, raises it to me again, and the rage is gone. Fully replaced with a smile.

"You know the thing you should be most afraid of out here?" he asks.

"You?" I ask.

"Mother Nature. She's the real bitch, and the snow is coming." He raises his palms to the sky and snow, as if on command, lands there. "It's gonna blizzard again."

"We're getting outta here."

"Hmm," he says, surveying the land around him. "Maybe, but not right now. Hey, you planning to drive out of that barn?" He pulls a set of keys out of his pocket and rattles them up at me. "That should be a neat trick."

George winces. Some part of him is hurting, shooting pain through him enough to make him stagger backward. He pulls himself together, but I see that it is still there in his stance, in his face, in the way he reaches out to the tree to prop himself up. He's weak.

The snow is coming down faster.

"I'll fucking kill you before you hurt anyone else."

"Good girl, stepping up like a real prince," he says. "Since you won't let me in, I'm going to go weather the storm elsewhere, but don't you fret. I'll be back as soon as I can."

I stand in the loft until George reaches the tree line. He doesn't try to hide his pain anymore, and as the wind picks up and pushes at him, he stumbles, falls into the snow, and then stands to give me a thumbs-up. Just before he disappears into the dark of the woods he turns and grins. It sends a chill through me.

"Emma," Earl says from below. "What are we gonna do?"

"Come here, Little Wing."

He climbs up to me. It is a long while before I can move my eyes off the space where George stood. The snow has begun to blow again, whipping white and thick and coming into the barn to beat at our faces. There is no walking out of this. Not now. Not yet.

When the tree line that enveloped George is no longer visible, Earl and I move down to the dim light of the first floor.

I drop to a seat on the ground in front of the woodstove and Earl climbs into my lap, wrapping his skinny body in mine. I hold him, his mask catching on the collar of my jacket.

"You've got to stop wearing this," I say.

I slowly remove the mask and for a moment he hugs me, presses his cheek to mine so I feel the bumps of what's been done to him. The skin is hard in a resilient way. He pulls away and offers me a smile that is so totally open and charming that I begin to cry.

"I'll put it back on." Earl reaches for his mask.

I swipe at my eyes, breathe.

"No," I say, and throw it into one of the barn's dark corners. "I'm sorry I started crying. I don't cry. Not much anyway." I hiccup. One hiccup. Two. The third one is loud, and I clamp my hand over my mouth. Earl laughs. That giggle. His face crinkles in a way far more genuine than the permanent wrinkles of his scars, and it makes me smile and hiccup again. We both laugh.

"I can't stop," I say.

"You have to hold your breath and roll your eyes," Earl says. "That's what my mom tells me."

"That's silly."

"Swallow the hiccup while it comes and keep rolling your eyes."

I try to do all these things, but Earl is laughing and then I'm laughing and then, at some point, the hiccups are gone.

"What are we gonna do?" he asks again.

"We're gonna wait until the snow eases up a bit and then we are going to drive right on out of here. Did you uncover the truck?"

"I did," he says, and points into the far dark corner of the barn.

Even in the dim light, I can tell that the vehicle with its nose nestled to the barn wall is something far better than the promised truck. I run to it.

"Earl! This is a 1986 Jeep Laredo. A CJ7."

"So?"

"The CJ2 was made in the forties. This is the same basic model, but the wheelbase on this sucker is, like, ten inches longer than that of the CJ2 or maybe the CJ5. They call them Willys."

"Okay . . . we can call him Willy if you want," Earl says. He's caught up with me to stand by my side.

The Jeep's door glides open. George has been lovingly caring for it. The interior is gorgeous. High-back leather bucket seats and a tilting steering wheel. It's a manual, five speed. I have to climb up into it; it's wonderfully tall. The tread on the tires is deep and thick and new.

Earl sidles up to the open door of the Jeep and is watching me admire the leather steering wheel.

"George loves this thing."

"Earl! This is amazing!" Earl just smiles at me like I'm crazy. "You don't get it at all, do you? This thing will bust through the barn door out into the snow. I bet it even has a winch on it that will help me pull Veronica out of here. Go look at the front. Is there a winch?"

"What's a winch?"

"Just see if there's a cable and a hook in the front."

Earl hustles around front, ducks down, and then rises back up with his thumb in the air.

"Go around," I yell. "Get in."

He climbs into the passenger side.

"See this?" I ask, pointing to a plaque on the dashboard.

He reads it slowly, stumbling a bit: "'Last of a Great Breed. This Collector's Edition CJ ends an era that began with the legendary Jeep of World War II.'"

"This is the real deal, Earl. This baby was probably made in my home state of Ohio. Unless that was just the diesel version made in Toledo . . . can't remember, but we couldn't have hoped for a better vehicle."

"A helicopter would be better," Earl says.

"Well, I guess! If you want to be all glass-half-empty. You did good, Earl. Bringing me here was supergood."

Earl giggles, pleased with himself. The feeling of a plan that might really work is intoxicating.

The Emma and Earl team might be the winning team after all.

"One problem," he says.

"No keys," I say, finishing the worry for him. "I've been known to jump-start a car or two. I'm sure I can do it."

"Really?"

"Really. We are going to bust old Willy the Jeep right through the damn barn wall."

"Fun!" he says, and claps his hands together in a way that reminds me he is just a little kid. "The storm will work through the night. We're safe in the barn."

"'Safe' is not a word I feel comfortable using in this place, but it would be good if you could rest a little. I can stay up and sit watch. If the snow stops, we'll have to get out of here. Daylight or no daylight. Let's go sit by the fire," I say, and we do.

I let my fears of George fade into the snowstorm and pull Earl onto my lap. We stare at the fire for a bit and then Earl twists to look up into my face.

"I love you, Emma."

He stares at me. His little sculptures, his forest mobiles, and marionettes. Hours of focus hiding in this barn, dodging around corners and staying in the dark. Days alone. Nights alone.

"What will I do with you?"

I rub at my face with both hands, and I wonder for the first time in days what I look like. It can't be good. Matted hair. Unwashed face. Evidence of sweat and vomit and blood. My scar throbs under my shirt. I haven't thought about Vicodin in a while, but it would be nice now. I took my own stitches out just before I met Lowell. Did it in a gas station bathroom with a pair of toenail clippers fresh out of the package. It hurt. Each loosening. Even with the meds. Each tug.

"I saw my mama go." He sits up and opens his palm. A small tinfoil object hangs from his finger in the breeze. It's the bird. My bird. It dances in the wind, his hand moving so gently that it's easy to ignore that it is Earl controlling the bird at all. It floats easily on the breeze, and with one sudden motion, the bird drops to the floor, loosed from his finger without warning. It sits in the dirt, lifeless. "She was all there. His hands were around her throat and her body was full and then nothing. Gone. George held on to her for days, crying and crying, but I knew it was okay. I saw her fly up and out before he took her down into the cellar. She got away from him no matter where he keeps her now." He pauses and takes a deep breath before sharing: "She's one of the crows now. The biggest of them."

I study his tiny, serious, scarred-up face. It gives away nothing. No sense of humor or awareness or irony.

"I can call her if you want. I'll show you."

"No, no. That's okay."

He shrugs and curls back up in front of the fire. I sit down behind him. Rub my hand over his back.

I take a deep breath and let the smoky warmth of the fire into my body. There was a winter with my father when we lived out of an old car someone never picked up from the garage. It was a 1980 B210 Datsun coupe. Navy. Almost brand-new but they'd wrecked it. My father put hours into making it right, only they never came back to pay their bill. It was around the same time that we lost the house. The first house. The one I was born in. There was a string of homes and apartments after that, but this was the first big loss, and from the way my mother tells it, my father decided on his own that losing our home was better than losing the garage.

Our furniture on the front lawn looked so meager and weak that we left most of it there. A sagging sofa. A tilted lamp. My mother screaming at my father as I held on to his hand. Then there was just Daddy and me at the garage. He pulled that Datsun into the shop and turned it into a bed for me. Lifted the hatch and filled the back with blankets. He slept up front in one of the bucket seats and told me stories until I fell asleep. All that shit happening around me and I was happy. He made me happy and he knew it. And yet it didn't stop him from leaving me.

For the first time, I wonder where my mother went during that time. I mean, I've thought about the fact that she didn't come with us before but more from the abandoned-child point of view. The why-is-she-so-mean-to-Daddy perspective. But what was it like for her? I remember, suddenly, going into the empty house to use the potty, but stopping because the bathroom door was cracked open and she was in there crying. Sobbing, really. She looked up at me as if I'd made a noise, although I swear I hadn't. Her eyes were red and swollen and there was snot on her upper lip and she said, "It'll be fine. Just give me a minute."

I said, “But I have to pee.” She stared at me like I was an alien. Looked at me with what I thought was hatred, and maybe it was. She left then. The bathroom. The house. Disappeared for days and I only remember thinking her selfish. Weak. A good mom would have stayed.

“You know, Earl, parents disappoint.” For a second, maybe two, I feel the relief of having said it, but then the relief is gone. So gone that the void fills with such a hot self-hatred that my hiccups start again, as if my body can somehow evacuate what I’ve just said. I was a cruel kid, a cruel teenager. And here I am . . . still selfish and still cruel.

“These hills are always shifting. Swallowing things up and then growing them anew. Life is cyclical. That’s what my mom says. We all come back,” he says, and then adds, “I’m sleepy.”

“Don’t fall asleep yet, Little Wing. Let’s pack what we can into the Jeep, all that stuff at the base of the ladder needs to go in, then we’ll check the weather again, and if it’s still bad out there, you can rest while I jump-start the Jeep.”

The snow is falling fat and fast when we are done loading up the Jeep. It is a white wall, a moat around our barn of a castle that allows us to relax a little, knowing George cannot get to us.

I walk over to the stove and lay down a blanket. “I’ll sit watch.”

He cuddles in beside me, flips and adjusts, flips and adjusts, rests his head on my leg.

"What would we do? I mean, if I decided to really leave here with you?" he asks.

"That's a good question."

"Could we get candy?"

I laugh.

"I like that one candy that comes in boxes."

"That describes a lot of candy, Earl."

"Ice cream! I want ice cream."

"Funny thing to want in the middle of a snowstorm."

"I can't sleep. I'm too waked up." He throws his arms over his face and then flops them at his sides. His scar doesn't look so bad in the firelight, the dramatic edges of it softened by the flickering shadows.

"Shut your eyes." I put my palm over his eyes. I move my hand up to his hairline and rub his temple. I smooth his scarred forehead and feel his body relax. "If you rest, we can head out of here whenever the snow lets up. It might even be safer to head out when it's still dark."

"Lemonheads," he mumbles.

"Good night, Earl," I answer.

"Night." He whispers the word back like it's an agreement between us.

I mean to stay awake. To keep watch over it all, and more responsibly, to listen for George to return, but the fire is warm and Earl's body trusts my body. We are two peas in a pod, and I am slipping, staying on the edge between sleep and wake. Pea Baby.

My mother stands over me with long brown hair stretching down to touch my face. She is all giggles and fairy dust. No, not fairy dust, she's crying. I shake myself awake, but I can see Earl's mother. She is naked. Her skin pale, her face flushed. She is beautiful until I get closer and see that her belly is cut open, marked with an *X*. Each flap of skin peeled back and inside there is a crow. A big black crow picking at her spine.

Wake up, Emma. Just wake up, but it is not Earl's mother at all. It's me. I'm the dead girl. The bird shifts, turns pink, rolls fetal. My never-baby gasping for air.

"He can't breathe," I say, but baby and body disappear.

I jerk awake.

The wind outside the barn is loud and whirring. The storm is still on and my eyes shut again. I think I should work on starting the Jeep but my body feels too heavy.

Time passes. The fire lights the darkness, throwing shadows that make me weary. "Help!" I shout from the deep black of a still dream. I sit up, hair stuck to my cheeks.

"Earl?" I fumble for him, but before my fingers find his leg, Earl shrieks. It's a shrill sound. With my hand on his calf, I feel the convulsions before I see his body thwap against the floor. Drool connects his mouth to barn dirt. His eyes are half open. His pupils have gone somewhere deep in his skull.

I saw a kid have a seizure in class once. Back in elementary school. He raised his hand, stood up from his desk, and then dropped to the floor and flopped around like a fish spilled out of its tank. No one did anything. Even the teacher, who was in his first year of teaching, did nothing. The kid, Nicholas, bit almost all the way through his tongue.

"Any idiot knows you put something in their mouth and keep their head from banging the floor," my father summed up for me after the incident.

I scan the room for something to fit in Earl's mouth before I realize the end of my leather belt will do. I whip it off. Earl is shaking, his arms curled up like a baby bird, his legs kicking violently, jostling me.

"You're okay." I keep my voice low and steady and put my hand between the top of his head and the floor to stop the thumping. I try to work the belt into his mouth but his jaw is locked. Teeth held tight to teeth. There is no blood so I wait what seems like forever for the shaking to slow. And it does. It slows, his jaw loosens, and there is no need for the belt.

"What's happening? Did I have a fit?" Earl finally wheezes. His eyes are bloodshot, one eyelid swollen just about shut.

"You had a seizure."

"Don't tell George." Earl is still breathing in gurgle spurts. He sounds like he's got a water fountain in his chest.

"Of course not." I smile to reassure him. "George isn't here. You're safe."

"I didn't use to do this. Mom says I was born normal, but when I was a little kid George hit me too hard. I only ever remember being like this."

"He caused them?" I'm aware of the volume of my voice but unwilling to let my anger drop. I feel it rising in my stomach, up to my chest and into my neck, tightening my hands into fists. I leap to my feet while Earl protests, wraps a thin hand around my ankle. He's weak. I don't even have to shake him off. The Jeep is on my right and the snow is piled high on the other side of the barn door. I pause with my palms on the wood. *What now, Emma? What you gonna do, Emma?* It's Ray's voice, teasing. Or it's Lowell's. *What the hell were you gonna do with a baby anyway, Emma?*

What am I going to do? Run through the snowstorm? Find George? Kill him?

I slam my fists into the door and then my boot. Beat at it until my foot breaks through the rotten wood and punches a small hole in the snow.

"Emma!" Earl twines his leg through mine and sends us both flying backward onto our butts. "You're making yourself bleed!"

We are both breathing heavily. I look at my hand. He's right. My knuckles are raw.

"I'm sorry, Earl," I manage. His arms are around my neck. *He* is comforting *me*. Sick. I'm truly and completely ill in the head.

"He was drunk that time. Mom didn't let him hit me again that hard. Not for years. Emma?"

"I hear you." I take a deep breath and turn to face him. "She should have taken you from him the first time he hurt you. You know that, don't you?"

"She did what she could," he says, and I wonder how this sweet little kid can be so kind to a mother who stood by and watched her husband beat him while I can't forgive my mother for moving on so easily after my father died.

"I'm not going to let him get you. Not ever again."

I lift my arms as if to ask his permission, and when he nods, I touch his face. I inspect all the scars up close with my eyes and my injured hands. I know I should speak, tell him it doesn't matter, that everything will be okay, but I can't.

"The scars will heal some." I smile.

"You think so?" Earl asks uncertainly, probably detecting my hesitancy.

"I know so," I say, mustering conviction. "It's gonna look manly." I wonder then, but do not ask, if he thinks of his genitalia as a kind of scar or wound that will not heal.

We lead each other back to the woodstove, and I let him sag loosely to the floor again where I cover him with blankets. I sit beside him holding his hand. His eyes slide shut, then he forces them open quickly to make sure I'm still there. "Sleep," I say.

"They make me tired." I know he means the seizures. Before Earl lets his eyes slide shut a final time he whispers, "I'm sorry."

I know the sound of that apology. He's apologizing for his father, for the shitty way in which he's been living, for the cold night, for his seizure, for his scars, for his girl body, for his entire life.

TWELVE

In the principal's office, there is a wide metal desk the color of the olives my mom likes to toothpick into her martinis, and a wall clock that marks the minutes with an angry thonk. The black arm makes its rounds as if carrying the weight of the world, each minute followed by a hefty and disgruntled sigh.

Ms. Latson sits on one side of the desk and I sit on the other. She's brought me in here before, although I've never done anything wrong. I am the type they like to keep a close watch on, alternating, I suspect, between fear I will stab someone and fear I will stab myself.

Rumor has it that no one other than Ms. Latson has ever been on the other side of that desk. Not even the janitorial staff is allowed back there and so students gossip endlessly about what might be in the five-foot space between her desk and the wall. Perhaps a bed with one sad blanket where she can curl up like a troll and sleep at night. Or that kid who never came back after freshman year, only hair, teeth, and fingernails left to reveal their identity.

There are photos on her desk, frames that carefully face her and only her so that delinquents like me cannot see who she is outside of this fucked-up place. Who is in those photos? Are they all photos of her? Are they her extended family? Photos of students from a long time ago when she liked her job?

The door to my left is clear glass. Mrs. Lowe and Scary Mary bustle around out there. They always look busy and annoyed but how hard can it be to take attendance and answer the phone? Students enter and leave the small space, shame heavy on their shoulders. None of this can be heard from where I sit. With the door closed, you enter a weird vacuum. An icebox of silence. The time bomb ticks, waiting for my story.

"What is it you need to tell me, Miss Powers? Take your time," she says, and yet there is no patience in her voice. "You called this meeting."

"Does one decide to be a high school principal or is it just something that happens to you?" I ask.

"Excuse me?" she asks. The clock quiets, skips a thonk.

"Did you always want to do this? Was it, like, your

dream? Other kids were all 'I want to be an astronaut, veterinarian, firefighter' and you were like 'I want to be a principal of a miserable high school.'"

"Oh," she says. The question bores her. "My father was a principal. You'll find that paths are often set for you before you realize. Not that my father told me I had to do this, but people tend to follow the paths they recognize."

"So you're saying I'm destined to be a drunk auto mechanic?"

"What? No." She is flustered now. She knows my backstory. Everyone does. "You can be whatever you want to be. That's why we are here, isn't it? To get a good education. To go on to college. Have you spoken with Ms. Zee?"

Ms. Zee is the guidance counselor. She is young and glows with an optimism that makes me feel sad. Students call her Cornbread for the sticky, flaky way she comes after all of us. Her good cheer so clingy, so messy.

"She doesn't like me," I say, and it's true. Cornbread has had no success breaking through my don't-give-a-shit exterior and it has begun to bother her. She recently recommended community college and then stumbled all over herself when I accused her of underestimating me.

"Well now, that's just not true. She likes everyone."

"She pretends to like everyone. There is a difference."

"Fine. It's almost final bell, Emma. Why are we here?" She slips her glasses off her nose, the left side catches on her ear for a second before it falls to her breasts, hung there by a silver chain so that she will never, ever lose them. She has brown eyes, crow's-feet at the corners.

"It's about Coach Matt."

"Okay," she says, and I can see she knows what's coming. Some version of it anyway. The bitch knows he's not right and has done nothing about it. I'm doing the right thing.

"He . . ." I pause for the show of it.

"You can tell me, sweetie," she says, but the affectionate nickname is not comfortable for her. "There are, of course, things I'd have to report. You understand that, right?"

"Like what?"

"Like if you tell me you are in danger or he is. If someone is a threat, it can't be kept secret."

I can see that she doesn't fully believe this is what I'm going to say. Maybe she doesn't know about the late-night, weed-riddled poker games or the rumors that he sleeps with all the girls. Maybe she isn't worried about his pretty face. Maybe she doesn't think I'm brave enough to speak truth and ruin a life.

"Is someone hurting you?" she asks.

"What?" Her question is a non sequitur. The "someone" part disconnecting it from Coach Matt in a way that I don't like. I'm about to say *This isn't about me* but then I realize what I see on her face is dread. She doesn't want to know. She wants me to keep it to myself.

I stare at her for a while and she lets me. There is still a chance I will say *Little Johnny cheated on a test* or *I've decided not to go to college* or *I've been cutting myself.* Any of these would be a brilliant alternative to what she worries is coming.

Her hands are folded on her lap where I can't see them.

I flick my eyes to the back of one of her framed photos. My arm reaches out before I give it permission to do so and latches on to the biggest frame. I pull it to me. Flip it around.

It's the beach. A stretch of it on either side of a boardwalk leading down to water so blue it doesn't look real.

"What is this?"

"Florida," she says.

I look at her and I can see she wants it back. That anything I tell her will slow down the time it takes for her to get out from behind that desk and into this photo.

She hates me. She hates all of us.

"Coach Matt touched me," I say.

"What do you mean 'touched' you?"

"He makes out with all the girls and I was over there and we got high and . . ."

"Over where?"

"His house."

"You were at his home?"

"I'm late," I say. "Two weeks."

This makes her stop breathing. The clock marks a

minute, two before she takes a deep breath. She puts her glasses back on as if there is something to see.

"Well, if this is true, we will need to call your mother. Get you to a doctor." It's a test. Maybe I'll back down.

"I don't want him to get in trouble."

"If what you are telling me is true, he is in trouble. He will be fired. Arrested, perhaps, if you want to press charges."

"Okay," I say quietly, as if I am sad for all of this. "No charges."

"That will be up to your parents. This isn't your fault, sweetie." The endearment comes out more genuine this time. She is thinking of me now. "He's young, but he's the adult. The teacher. It's his responsibility to know better."

"Okay," I say again.

"How many other girls?" she asks. The situation is unfolding before her now. She sees how bad this is going to be. "Will others come forward?"

"I don't think so. Does anyone have to know it was me that talked? Besides my mother, I mean."

"I should tell Ms. Zee. Can I get her? Yes, that would be the best next step. Let me get her in here and you two can talk it through."

"Ms. Zee hates me," I say.

"She does not." Ms. Latson is already up and walking to her office door. Her relief about getting away from me is palpable.

The door shuts behind her. I am left alone in the icebox of an office. I wait a clock beat, two, and then three before I stand and move to her side of the desk. I sit in the office chair, feel the indent of her butt under mine. I pull myself up to the desk. She has five frames. Two are of a beach scene. One is old. Her and her parents, perhaps. The other two are empty. The frames are ornate, silver, one has a turquoise stone at the bottom. The black mat of the frame shows through. No picture. A sign of an empty life. Either that or she has already begun to slowly move out, disappearing her life one picture at a time.

I open the middle drawer, a single pencil rolls forward. Three paper clips sit rusting. How does one measure a life? Half empty? Half full?

I stare into the drawer and the sadness in me grows. Blooms huge in my heart, the lie I'm telling growing, stretching its blue veins through my body.

"What did you do, Emma?"

Ray is standing over me. He's crying and I can't remember what I've done right away, although I know I've done something. He's woken me from a deep sleep. I was having a nightmare or what seemed to be a nightmare. I wasn't scared. In it, I was a house. Tall windows for eyes, a spiral staircase up one leg through my torso into the attic of my heart. Inside someone is banging at me to get out. They have a hammer in their hand and it hurts, purple bruises spread with each hit and the sound is familiar. The hit thudding like a big black minute hand shifting into the future. Thonk. Thonk. Thonk.

"I'm sleeping, Ray," I say. "Go away."

"He's gone."

"He who?" I ask, and now I'm awake. It's been a week since I reported Coach Matt. Since Cornbread got to do her best job ever, making me process the proper emotions. Calling my mother in so we could tell her together. When Ms. Zee left us alone, she said, "Jesus, Emma. I wanted better for you."

"I don't *know* that I'm pregnant."

"Easy to find out."

"I went to his house last night and everything was gone. Everything."

"Who's gone?" I ask, buying time.

"Coach Matt! You're the only one who knew," Ray says.

"He was hurting you," I say.

"That's not what you saw and you know it."

"Oh, ick. Not that. He is your teacher. He was twenty-something. It's against the law."

"Did you tell them you caught us having sex? Is that what you told them?"

This is not what I told them, but I want to hurt Ray. Even as he sits in front of me hurting, I want to hurt him more so I lie.

"I told them he was molesting you. That he was gay and you were scared."

"Jesus, Emma."

"What? How is that not true?"

"Does my dad know?"

"Know what?"

"That I'm gay!"

"You're not gay," I say. It isn't something I've even considered. Not really. Ray loves me. I love Ray. We will be together forever. "Please. I have gay friends. You are not gay."

"Emma," he whispers. His sadness is deeper than I realized. It is shrinking him. His chin to his chest. His arms curling into his torso. A little crippled thing. "You know me. You know this about me."

"He made you think you're gay."

"Emma! Don't be so fucking stupid! I loved him. I love him, and he's gone!" Ray screams louder than I've ever heard him scream. He screams until his voice won't let him scream anymore and his arms begin to scratch, rip at the soft skin on the insides of his arms.

"Ray! Stop it. I'm sorry." I try to grab his wrists but he won't let me get to him and then he is on top of me, holding me down so I can't move.

"You are selfish like your mother. An addict like your father," he says in a voice so calm that I believe him.

"I love you, Ray. You are my best friend."

He smacks me then. Hits my face hard. My eyes blur

with tears and I stare up through the haze into his face. Our eyes locked to each other and I see how much he hates me. I've never seen that look on his face before.

"Fine, you're a fucking faggot."

I've never said the f-word before and it startles us both.

"I'm not a faggot," he says. His arms weaken and I flip him on his back.

I'm selfish. I'm psycho.

I kiss him and he kisses me back as if it is a dare. I know what we will do next to prove to ourselves what we are and what we are not, and even in the moments when I know I want to stop it, I don't. I let it roll. The beasts of us both crawling out into the light.

THIRTEEN

"Whatcha doing?" a sleepy Earl asks from the top rung of the ladder. He's climbed up to find me in the loft. The sky is clear, pink with the sunrise, and the wind stopped howling maybe an hour ago.

"Looking for footprints. I want to make sure we're the only people here."

Earl stands next to me. The wind has pushed the snow into waves that break thickly against the trunks of the pine trees. Earl's crows have come. Gathered in the top of one of the far trees. Their black bodies heavy against the white.

"George will be back soon," he says. "Eat something."

Earl hands me a sleeve of saltines. They are stale, but the salt is welcome, and I eat several.

The crows begin to take off from the tree as we watch. Their caw-caw is only slightly louder than the noise of their wings against the frozen South Dakota air. They are large birds, but one is decidedly larger, its wingspan is quite grand, and it leads the flock, six of them circling before disappearing over the top of the barn, reappearing to complete their circle.

"The brain of a crow is exactly the size of a human thumb," Earl says, and holds his thumb up as if to measure it against the crow. "If you look at it in relation to their head and body, it's pretty big."

"They are flying garbage eaters," I say as I remain focused on the tree line. *Where are you, George?*

I've turned toward the ladder so my back is to Earl when he screams. I spin to see that a crow has come through the opening and landed on him. Its claws in his hair, its beak pecking at his face. The big black oil slick of a bird holds tight to Earl's head and pushes his beak down over Earl's face. Something splashes my cheek. I wipe it away. Blood.

"Hey!" I scream, waving my arms wildly and stepping into the fray. An outstretched wing hits me in the throat. The muscled strength of it staggers me.

"Drop the crackers!" I yell at Earl. *Crows*, Ray once told me, *are highly intelligent, omnivorous, and adaptable. They will survive anywhere. Eat anything.* I rip off my jacket and start swinging it at the bird. It squawks and launches itself into the sky.

Earl's back is to the outside world, his heels teetering on the edge of the hayloft. For a second, Earl looks like he will find balance, but that moment is gone and Earl is falling backward.

"Earl!" I drop my jacket and run to peer over the edge. Earl is on his back in the snow. "Are you okay?"

Before he can answer the crows are dive-bombing him. Swooping down but not landing, working up their nerve to dig their claws in. I jump, landing in the snow next to Earl and then roll onto him so that my body is over his. I gather him up under me. Crows land on my back. They knead their claws into the cotton of my shirt, as if they imagine themselves cats. Their talons poking their needle marks into my skin. One takes off before the other. The remaining crow stands on my back. Its body heavy as a boulder. In the sky, a fellow crow calls for it, and eventually, it lifts off. I wait, counting to a hundred before I loosen my grip on Earl and look up to the sky.

The birds are gone.

Blood trickles down from his hairline, and I dig through his hair to find deep cuts.

"You like those things, huh?"

"She doesn't recognize me without my mask."

"Who doesn't recognize you?"

"Mom. She'd never hurt me on purpose."

I hold my T-shirt to his forehead.

"She never saw me with these—these—umm," he stammers, "these bad spots." He is referring to his scars. "She only knows me now with the mask on."

"Be real with me for a second, Earl. Animals do what they need to do to survive and the snow came early. They are just scared and hungry."

"I'll put my mask back on so she can tell it's me."

The blood seeps up to the surface of his face, volcanic. Stitches would be good, but they aren't going to happen.

"You are not to wear that mask or any mask ever again. This is you. You do not hide," I say, and press the cloth to his scalp. We stare at each other. His green eyes are on mine. "Your mother would say the same thing if she were alive."

He breaks my gaze. Looks away from me into the snow.

"Your mother is gone, Earl. There's nothing we can do about that."

I wait for him to speak, to look back up at my face, but he won't, and it's too cold to wait for an epiphany. Earl's ears are already harsh with pink and my hands burn.

"Good morning." A sound to eclipse the birdcalls. "How did everyone sleep?"

George stands at the tree line, not fifty yards away, with red gas cans in his hands.

Earl begins to breathe too fast, wheezing within seconds.

"Get back inside," I say. Earl does not move. "Now! Climb!" My shout wakes him into movement, and I stand between George and the climbing trees.

"What's the deal with being so fucking psycho, George? Can't you just do your thing and we'll do ours?"

George moves slowly forward. His hurt arm can barely hold up the gas can. It drags the left side of his body closer to the snow.

"Don't worry," he says. "I'm determined, but I'm a slow mover. Go on. Go back inside with my offspring. It'll take me a minute to get the flames going."

Earl's boots are disappearing into the hayloft as I begin my tree climb. George makes it to the barn and is unscrewing the lid of one of the red gas cans at the same time that I'm stepping off the climbing trees and into the hayloft.

"Settle in. Eat breakfast. I'll take my time." He splashes some gas up onto the barn. "Oh, wait," he says, and sets down the can. "I should show you this too. From inside his jacket, he displays a rifle. He's got it somehow attached to his waist so it moves with him as he walks, a third limb. "I'm good with it. I can shoot real straight."

"Fantastic," I say. Earl is just behind me, his breath still coming quickly.

"Just want you to know what you're up against. Of course, if you want to walk out of here, I'm good with that too. Just leave me my kid."

"Emma," Earl whines from below.

"Shhhh," I hiss into the dark of the barn.

"Don't leave me, Emma. He'll kill me," he says. Earl's voice echoing up from the depths of the barn.

"Jesus, I'm not going to fucking leave you," I say. "We're going to make it out of here. You and me. Just get back." I step out of George's sight and climb down the ladder to join Earl. "Get in the Jeep."

"But we don't have keys."

"Doesn't matter. I just need a knife."

In the driver's seat, I pry back the panel under the steering column. The mess of green and red and black wires spill out as I knew they would.

"My father taught me how to hot-wire cars. It's stupid easy. I just need this switchblade."

The dim light makes it difficult, but the red and the black wires are there. I strip the ends of both, then hand the blade to Earl.

"Keep that with you," I say, and then ask, "Ready?"

"Ready."

Copper to copper and the engine purrs to life.

"Cool," Earl says, and I do feel cool. I am something George isn't expecting.

I twist the wires together and put Willy in reverse. I back up twenty feet before I hit Earl's art table and then I go back farther, mumbling sorry to Earl as I hear the table scrape against the bumper.

"We're going through?" he asks. "For real?"

"For real," I say. "Seat belt on?"

"On."

"Lock your door."

"Locked."

"Here we go."

I push the accelerator to the floor and we shoot forward, wood splinters around us. I lose my nerve for just a second and let up on the gas. We stall out. The front bumper raised high on a combination of splintered barn wood and South Dakota snow.

I put the Jeep in reverse again. We move backward smoothly. Next I slide us into first, second, and then we shoot through the rubble of the barn and out onto the snow. The gas pedal to the floor as we climb into the daylight.

I'm shifting into third when Earl screams.

The Jeep hits something solid. My head bangs the steering wheel and then swings back to hit the headrest, and my neck makes a funny snap of a noise. Blood oozes from a cut on my forehead and slides into my right eye. I feel fuzzy. I move my head cautiously to look at Earl, but his sweet face slides away from me, telescoping back, back, back.

"I'm okay," I mumble, but then it is completely dark.

The world turns to velvet, and in the dark, I hear only Earl.

"You can start an avalanche by stepping in the wrong

place," Earl says. And I see snow all around me where there is supposed to be a Jeep. I am standing on the train tracks. The rails frozen. If I move my body at all I will slip and bang my head. The scene changes.

I am outside the diner. The lights inside are flickering. Veronica is parked where we left her, buried to the doors in snow. Birds are piled up on the ground beside her—four birds, no, six—huddled on top of something. One of them tilts its head toward me, and even though they are far away and I am silent, I know the bird is looking me over with one eye and then the next.

Suddenly Earl is next to me, holding my hand, and the crow raises her beak to the sky and caws, loud as a scream. She calls up and out, alerting the world to something fierce and carnal and angry.

The bird that began the chorus stops abruptly, ruffles its body as if cold, and launches itself into the sky. In its wake, I see what it was hiding with its dark feathers. A pale ankle, a delicate foot. The woman from the cellar. She is naked, skin welted with red. Her black hair hangs as dark as the crows' feathers over her bare breasts.

"It's my mother," Earl says in a far-off voice that makes me feel very sad.

Then he is in her lap, or what would be a lap if she were sitting up. He is wrapping his arms around her, squishing himself to her bare chest.

"Earl, honey, get away from the bird," I say.

She sits up. Her eyelids close and then open again to take me in.

"Hello," she says. She looks at me, black eyes that seem to be nothing but pupil, and I lunge for Earl.

I jolt back into my body, breathing hard. I cannot see out of my left eye. It's swelling shut.

"Emma, Emma!"

We are in the Jeep. My head is bleeding. I've hit it on the steering wheel. A crow sits on the hood of the Jeep. Earl's mother. She peers at us. Pecks at the glass.

A noise, loud and fierce as a thunderclap and the window next to Earl's head explodes.

"Fuck!"

I restart the Jeep, press too hard on the gas, and we lurch forward. Almost stalling again.

"Go right!" Earl is yelling, and for a moment, I can't recall what right is but then we're curving around the barn, finding a path free of trees that is wide enough for the Jeep. We drive fifteen miles per hour, twenty. I hear another gunshot and another. The bullets do not reach us.

"You can go slow, Emma. He's hurt. He won't be able to keep up."

"Where's your mother?"

"What?"

My thoughts are confused. My head aches.

I am in the diner kitchen. The swinging door between the eating area and the prep room is frantically swinging.

"Emma!"

I am driving the Jeep. Up the hill, through the trees to the ghost town.

"Are you okay?" Earl puts his hand on the steering wheel.

In the diner kitchen, the bird woman faces the stove. There are two wounds between her shoulder blades, slashes so deep and thick that I see muscle. In spite of their depth, their plant-pulled-up-by-the-roots severity, they are not bleeding. They expose the red and pink of her insides. Two spaces awaiting the perfect planting.

The bird woman straightens her back, rolls her shoulders, and the holes gape and yawn. She does not turn to face me.

"Who's in the cellar?" I ask.

"We all come back," the bird woman says, and then the snow is before me, the broken farmhouse straight ahead.

"You're scaring me," Earl says, and my body goes limp. The Jeep lurches forward and stalls out. I'm going to be sick. I open the door and vomit into the snow. I shut my eyes and behind the lids I see the crow woman.

"He's been calling your name for days," the crow woman says.

"If he's still alive, we need to get him out of the cellar."

"I know. I'll go get him."

"No!" I yell, but Earl is already outside the car, making his way through the snow. I need to wake up. My brain is bruised. If I don't shut my eyes, I will regain focus. I'll ground myself in the here and now. I step out of the Jeep. The ghost town stares at me; the farmhouse gapes.

I move more quickly than I think possible. I turn the corner of the house and there is Earl, already removing a long metal pipe that George has jammed through the door handles. Not so far off in the woods there is a gunshot, a whoop of victory.

"Wait!" I yell at Earl, and he stops and turns back to me.

I make the mistake of pausing. Just for a second. My eyes shut and the bird woman is there, pointing down the cellar steps. She holds her arm steady in the air. She is still naked. Her body is covered with little bumps of skin that are mounding up.

"You've left a lot unfinished," she says to me. "These things do not like to be unresolved."

"Stop it. Just stop it," I say. I shake myself awake even though it hurts.

A sound comes now from a long way off. A baby crying. An infant ragged with cold and fear. The sound comes through the woods, closer and closer. I cover my ears, but then it's inside of me. Rising up from my middle to scream inside my head.

FOURTEEN

Emma," Earl is saying. "Emma!" I press my hands tight to my head and tighter still. I want to press so hard that my skull collapses, but I am weak and my eyes leak water. The baby's cries get louder until I open my eyes, and there is Earl. The shape of him is blurry through tears and his mouth is changing, widening into a gaping hole, too big to be real, but the sound is real. That loud baby cry is crinkling his face, exploding out of him. He will swallow me.

"Stop!" I yell. "Stop! Stop! Stop!" I push at my ears. The sound does stop, and the absence of it is so peaceful and complete that I begin to weep. I speak again between gulps for air. "I'm sorry. Sorry, sorry, sorry, sorry, sorry."

I say it so much that it doesn't sound like a word anymore. Earl's hands are on my arms, pulling my palms from my ears. I open my eyes and there he is. His sweet melty face looking at me.

"It's okay," he says.

"I just wanted to go to sleep, Earl."

"Huh?" Earl asks.

I've said *wanted*. Past tense. I'm thinking of Emma and Ray. Ray and Emma. Of how hard those two tried to go to sleep. To cease to be awake.

"I'm so tired," I say.

"You can't go to sleep."

"I wanted him to love me," I say. My words slur. "A baby would have made us into something."

"Stay here with me," he says. "Don't go away again."

The crow woman is here.

I ask her: "How does this end?"

"Who told you it had an end?" she asks.

"Everything has an end. A beginning, middle, and end. That's basic shit," I say. "You're born. You live. You die."

"It isn't like that. It's cyclical." She cocks her head to the right. "You begin, you begin, you begin. Or you end, you end, you end. Either way there is no stop. No go."

"I don't believe you," I say. My brain is tired and sad and so, so foggy. I'm slogging through snow, dragging my feet from one deep hole into the next.

She does not answer but tilts her head the other way. I look at her tiny cuts, hundreds of them, all over her naked body suddenly budding with black, feathers peeking out from inside and coming to the surface like shoots of grass.

"I want to begin," I say, swallowing bile.

"Emma," Earl says, and wraps his arms around me.

He tilts his sweet face to mine. He is a thousand years old. Indefinite suffering sits in his ragged scars, his crooked teeth, but he is also a little boy. I want to keep him. Save him.

"What do I do?"

"He's coming," Earl says.

A bullet smashes into the Jeep.

Earl and I are at the cellar door. I pull the metal bar the rest of the way out and we swing the doors open together. In the dark, on the bottom stair there is a body. Curled into a ball. Only the hard shell of its back is showing.

"Lowell," I call down into the abyss.

My mind is suddenly sober. I wipe blood from my eyebrow before it drips into my eye.

"We need a flashlight," I say to Earl.

"It's in the Jeep. You want me to get it?"

"Hell no. You stay as close to me as you can."

"Lowell Smith! It's Emma Powers. I need to hear you're alive."

Lowell uncurls slowly. The ridge of his back straightening out. Once he's unrolled, he puts his back to the cellar dirt and covers his eyes to guard against the bright daylight we've shone down his hovel hole.

"Fuck you," he says, his voice soft with hurt.

"Can you walk?" I ask.

"It's so dark. I've been making my dying plans with the old lady and the others."

"Jesus Christ. I have to go down and get him," I say, and start down. First foot on the first step, but Earl grabs my arm. "Is he worth saving, Emma?"

"No," I say without pause and then think but do not say, *But maybe I am.*

The climb down into the cellar seems short this time. Earl follows closely behind me. I can smell Lowell. That specific smell of him mixed with blood and piss and decay. At the base of the steps, there is darkness. I do not look around for the others. I already know they are there.

"I have a Jeep. It'll get us out of here and off the mountain, but we have to move now."

"I'm not going anywhere with you," he whispers.

"Don't be stupid, Lowell. Why would I come down here just to hurt you?"

"Again. Hurt me again."

"Whatever. As if you weren't going to hurt me. As if you hadn't already."

"I was fucking nice to you. But you're right. I do want to hurt you," he says savagely, swinging for my ankle.

I step easily away.

"Too slow," I say.

"There's a body down here," he says. "I can't get close to it but I think it's been down here awhile."

"I know," I say.

"Fantastic. I was just planning what position I'd like to be found in. Replaying *Mother's Milk* song by song in my head. I can't remember track three, but I got all the rest just about perfect."

"Can you move?"

"I'm not as whole as I used to be. You shot me. That's what started it off. You evil fucking cunt."

"Don't call her that!" Earl says, starting to move between me and Lowell.

"Ladies," George says from the top of the cellar steps, blocking most of the light. "It's nice of y'all to consolidate yourselves. I'll ask you to sit tight and let me take care of what I need to. Should be over in no time."

I rise to my full height and make a move for the stairs. He holds the barrel to my face. I have Lowell's gun in my jacket pocket. No bullets, but it's there. The threat of it could be helpful, but it's zipped into my inside pocket and will take too long to reach.

"I can shoot you now if you want," George says, thrilled with himself.

"Go for it," I say. "I die down here now or you die later when I get out."

My willingness to be shot in the face catches him off guard. Rattles him a little, and his trigger finger twitches.

Fuck it, I think, but not fast enough. He steps back and slams one cellar door shut and then the other. There is the noise of the pipe sliding into place right before the sound of my hand banging on the metal door.

"George!" I shout.

The fear is instant and full and real. The dark of the cellar so complete that it seems it's all I have. The dark and the fear. Ghosts rise up from behind me, and they mean me harm. Ray. My dad. Earl's mother.

A hand closes around my ankle. I scream and bang my head on the metal doors above me, hard. My already bruised brain softens a little more. The ringing in my head brings the baby cry back. So loud and close that I touch my belly to make sure the baby isn't right here with me.

"Don't worry. He's locked me down here plenty," Earl says.

The baby quiets to a whimper.

"That's fucking nuts," Lowell says, and releases my ankle. "I'll kill you once we're out of this mess."

"Sure you will," I say, and step past him.

Earl leads me carefully down the stairs farther into the dark past his mother. Lowell stays where he is at the foot of the stairs. The four of us tucked away in our new hell.

"I know how to get out. I've done it plenty of times," Earl says.

"I've army crawled all over this place," Lowell says. "There's no way out except the doors."

My eyes are adjusting to the dark and my hearing is sharpening. Earl is moving away from me, deeper into the cellar.

"Anyone locked up down here for very long is likely crazy," Lowell whispers.

"No worse than either of us."

"Well, that's not saying much."

"Earl?" I ask.

"I'm here."

His voice comes through from a ways away. The space is not large but the darkness hangs between us like a wall. I know reaching him would take quite some time.

"There are loose bricks," he says. "In the chimney. I know how to climb up."

I walk back to Lowell but keep my distance. He's crazy enough to change his mind and yank me down onto the dark cellar floor with him.

"I don't want to leave you here. Let's see if you can stand."

He wheezes as he tries to sit and then gives up.

"Fucker bandaged my leg and fed me. Then he hit me over the head. I was down here when I came to."

"How's the leg?"

"Where you shot me, you mean? Bullet seems to have gone through."

"We gotta go," Earl says suddenly, right next to us.

"Help me get him up, Earl."

"No point. He won't fit up the chimney. Neither will you. There's a patch of loose bricks at the base. It's tight, but I can climb up the inside and come out the fireplace upstairs. I'll go up and come around to let you out. And I don't think you should go near that man. He wants to hurt you."

"Kid has a point," Lowell says.

"We're not separating," I say.

"Emma."

"Earl."

"I'll be quick. As long as we get to the Jeep, we will make it out."

"No."

A smell comes then. Melting down from above. Something familiar and yet I don't know what it is right away. A waft of it blows through the dark space and my father's garage comes alive. The young men who used to work for him. Chris was the youngest and always wore a ball cap. The guy named Jacob who got fired for skimming the register but then rehired because my dad said he was too much like him at twenty to be held accountable. The oil-slick concrete. The noise of the lifts.

"Jesus, is that gasoline?" Lowell asks. George is above us, wetting the floorboards. I hear, but do not feel, drops coming down and hitting the ground around us.

"I'll be back. Wait on the steps," Earl says.

My eyes have adjusted enough that I can see Earl's shape moving into the dark.

"I don't like this!" I shout.

A few drops hit the top of my head. The boards creak under George's feet, and I wish I could punch through the floor and drag him down with us.

"He gonna fucking burn us alive?" Lowell asks.

"Seems that way."

"Holy fuck."

"Holy fuck," I repeat.

"You gotta move," I say, and we set about the struggle of standing him up. We hobble up one step, two. Then rest.

"Why would you come back to help me?"

"Whisper," I say. "He's right up there." We can hear George humming.

"He knows we're down here. He put us here. Why'd you come get me?"

"I'm tired of running."

Above us there is a thump, but over that George is hollering. Words I can't make out, but he is definitely stomping his feet. Pounding on the floor above us. The smell of gasoline is getting stronger.

"Burn!" George screams. One distinct word and then a whoosh that reminds me of a furnace kicking on. The space around us brightens, a glow passing down through the boards above us.

"It's lit," Lowell says.

I resist the urge to call Earl's name.

"He'll come for us," I say to Lowell. "He'll open the door and we'll get to the Jeep. It's not far."

"I can't move. I can't make it up the stairs."

Smoke filters down. The smell of it stronger than the smell of the gas. Toxic. Thick.

"You can. You need to try."

Lowell nods and together we get him up one stair, then the next.

"Press your face to the doors. The crack. Get air."

I bury my nose and mouth in the elbow of my jacket. The chimney is visible now from where we stand. Bricks loosed from the base where Earl slipped in. His mother's legs visible on the other side. I'm watching when she lights up. A small cinder drops onto her leg and what's left of her catches quickly, burns fast, as if she's been waiting for it. A new smell fills the room. Burning hair, skin, and fingernails.

"Holy fuck," Lowell says, removing his face from the crack of air and pressing me to it. I take three gulps and move him back.

She's lit up now like a bonfire. The lit gasoline and broken splinters of wood are otherwise dropping down and fading out in the cold, half-frozen puddles of the cellar floor, but she, Earl's mother, is burning.

The cellar doors fly open. The world is bright and oxygen floods in. The flames behind us leap for us but miss. Lowell stumbles into the snow, and I follow.

"Hurry," Earl says. "He knows I'm out."

The Jeep is right where we left it. The glass is shattered but the tires are whole and full.

"He won't make it," Earl says, nodding at Lowell.

"Maybe I can drag him. Earl, turn on the Jeep. Get in and open the door for us."

Earl does as I say.

The old house fully ignites, shoots up hot flames and George steps out onto the porch.

"Don't you leave me, you fucking bitch," Lowell says. Behind us I see George raising his rifle to shoot.

"Lowell!" I shout his name as one of George's bullets rips through his skull. Lowell's eyes are still on me when his body flops to the cellar stairs, his fingers are the last things I see as gravity pulls him underground and into the fire.

I turn to the Jeep and run.

"Shut the doors!" I scream to Earl and listen to them slam as I reach the driver's side and slam my door too. I turn the Jeep on and it revs up.

George is coughing. The fire creeping up on him too. The smoke finding its way to his lungs. "Belt in," I say to Earl.

For a second, I look out the shattered windshield and straight at George.

He raises his rifle before I press on the gas, turning swiftly away from him, and a bullet whizzes through the Jeep, close and fast.

"Go right!" Earl shouts. His hands clutch the dash. There's a snowmobile trail the Jeep can handle, and we crash through brush and snow, rocks and pine trees coming close enough on either side to scrape the Jeep, but I drive on.

FIFTEEN

The world bumps and flashes by outside the Jeep. Earl has turned on the heat full blast but the wind whips in the windows to chase it away as soon as it leaves the vents.

"There," Earl says, pointing ahead. I don't see anything at first but then there's the shine of the diner. The wide white expanse of its parking lot opens up in front of us. Veronica. *I'm here, baby girl.* The snow has tried to swallow her, but she hasn't given in. Her burnt orange armor shines through the snowdrifts.

The front of the Jeep faces the front of Veronica.

"I'll leave the Jeep running," I say. Earl and I step out of the Jeep and sink in up to our ankles. "Do you know how to make it work?" Earl asks, looking at the tight coil of a steel cable.

"In theory," I say. Veronica's bumper kisses the top of the snow. "Problem is if I can dig her out enough to hook her to the winch, we are going to do a ton of damage getting her up and over the snow." I put my palm on Veronica's snout. "How long do we have before George arrives?" I ask Earl.

Earl does not answer.

When I turn to him, I see that his legs are shaking from the bottom up like a slow-growing earthquake. The shaking moves into his torso, his arms, his neck, and head, and then it stops completely, giving me enough time to whisper his name before he collapses. His limbs pooling loosely around him in the snow.

Once on the ground Earl doesn't move, not even a twitch, but the white-white snow surrounding him gains depth and texture. Earl's dirty-blond hair spaghetti thick and sticky.

I move forward and kneel down to him quickly, scanning the forest for George.

Earl's eyes flick open, but my face does not register in his pupils. There's spittle bubbled up at the corners of his mouth, and he makes soft sounds, barely even groans. I brush his hair off his forehead.

"Earl? Can you hear me?"

I pat Earl's cheek, finding only scabs. Remnants of his

former self. When they fall off, he'll snake-shed his past. Start again.

Earl's hand closing over mine startles me, and I meet his suddenly wide-open eyes.

Earl opens his mouth to speak, but the noise that comes out is garbled and painful to hear. He puts his hand to his throat.

"Can't talk?" I ask. "You got your tongue this time?"

I help him around to the side of Veronica, unlock the passenger door and lift him inside. "Just shut your eyes for a minute." Earl shakes his head no but then shuts his eyes anyway. He coughs, a small drop of blood leaks out of the corner of his mouth.

"Open up. Wide." Earl does as told. His mouth is full of blood and saliva. "Spit, come on. Into the snow. Lean forward. Now spit." I shift to support Earl's weight so he can dribble red into the snow. It splashes back onto my hand hot. "Don't you worry," I say. "We'll stay right here until you feel a little better."

Earl coughs again, this time I hear a small squeak escape. I wipe the blood from the corners of his mouth.

"Let me put a little snow on your tongue. It'll keep down the swelling." I slide in a small amount, and Earl winces, then swallows. I repeat it, and this time Earl holds it in his mouth to let it melt before he spits out a hot wad of bloody snow and phlegm. "Open again."

Earl does as he is told and sticks out his tongue. It's

mangled, but not so much from recent events. He's bitten into the left side. His molars leaving their almost-perfect indentations.

A gunshot. Loud and booming. Earl and I both jump.

A second shot. This time I hear it hit something with a thwap.

"Get in," I say, pushing Earl into the van and stepping in beside him. I slam the door shut behind us.

Earl makes a scribbling gesture with finger to palm.

"A pen?"

Earl nods yes. I move up to the front of the van. George is a dark shape against the brilliant snow, gun pointed at the sky. He's standing still at the tree line, bulking himself up.

I rip open the glove compartment, letting the door slam down with a thunk. I dump its contents onto the floor until I find a scrap of paper and a pen. Earl writes quickly. I take the paper back. Hands steady. Earl's written: *Do you know to use the gun?*

He's left out the word "how," but it doesn't matter. I know what he's asking.

"I can, but there are no more bullets so it hardly matters."

Bullet in the diner, he writes.

"No way. Why didn't you say?"

He shrugs.

I'm almost mad, but I can't think of what that would

accomplish. I pull the formerly useless gun from my own pocket and examine it.

"How do you know the bullets will even fit this gun?" I ask.

He writes: *I stole some from you.*

"Where are they?" I ask, but move back to the front seat before he can write an answer. George is coming toward the Jeep. He's lowered the rifle in front of him and moves grudgingly through the snow. One heavy foot lifted then sunk back in then lifted again. He does not move with any sort of ease but he is still terrifying. The hulk of him defying injury.

Earl rattles his scrap of paper at me until I take it: *Baking cupboard.*

"The bullet is in the baking cupboard? I don't know where that is."

He points toward the diner, impatient.

"I know it's in the diner. I just don't know where the baking cupboard is." I turn my attention back out the window. He will be to the Jeep soon. And then what? He'll shoot Earl? He'll take the Jeep? Nothing good will come of it.

Earl is nudging me, impatient. "We need a plan," he says, managing to form sounds close enough to words.

"Here," I say. "You have the switchblade? Take the gun too and run for the diner. I'll distract George. Go now." Earl shakes his head no so I move around him, throw open the side door so the snow and cold whirls in fresh around us. "It's a straight shot to the door," I say, and it is. Van door to diner door to baking cupboard. George is on the other side, attention focused on the Jeep. Earl will make it, just.

Earl shakes his head no again so I pry open his fingers, plant the gun in his palm, and push him out into the snow.

"Run! Now!" I push back to the front of the van and get in the driver's seat. I lay on the horn. *Good job, Veronica*, I think. This is it. The sound is certain, loud, and George turns his attention from the Jeep windows to me. I honk once more, then wave, a friendly little hello as if this is all just me trying to say hello.

George waves back. A grim little wave that ends with a smile.

"Shit," I say. He lowers the rifle and shoots before I can duck. The bullet hits the windshield. Glass sprays inward, the shards sparkling brighter than the snowflakes and clouding my vision before I can cover my face with my arms.

I am blind. I drop between the two front seats and begin to crawl toward the back, to where the air is entering the van. The glass crunches under my palms and sticks to my skin, some of it shaking off to salt the floor again. The world is dark and I move by feeling. Glass shards cutting palms easing into the metallic floor of the van. My knees bang the metal and the cold air whooshes in through the side of the van telling me I am close and then I am stumbling out. The snow feels like a blessing on my wounds and I bury my face in it. Let it settle into a mold before I pull back an inch and try to open my eyes. They burn and blur. The snow looks red but that could be a trick of the light of my mind. I can see well enough to move so I am up, launching myself toward the diner, toward Earl.

"Stop." It's one word. Just the one but I hear everything in it. His intent. His sense of righteousness. His willingness to do whatever feels like the next right step.

I stop.

"Turn toward me."

I turn toward the sound of his voice. My vision is blurred, tear-filled but both eyes working. He is a lump of a man. A gruff shape come to find me.

"What the fuck do you want?" I ask.

"What do you think I want? My kid. My Jeep. My damn dignity back."

"You'll have to shoot me then," I say.

My body aches.

"Where's my kid?"

"Not here."

"Liar," he says.

I sway, afraid I'll vomit again. He lowers his rifle, then hangs it over his shoulder. Lets it swing there freely. Flaunting.

He stands in front of the diner door, backed up to it with his grim face still aimed at me when he says, "This is my home. You leave now on your own or you leave dead." He turns quickly and is disappearing inside the diner, shoving the stubborn diner door closed.

Rage races from my tailbone to my neck.

I'm not fucking afraid of you. I stride toward the diner. Take the steps in one stretch and throw my side into the door. It bangs open and I'm suddenly right behind him. He spins on his heels to face me and we're close now. I inch my foot forward, just so he knows I'm not afraid to walk through him. He's doing it. Folding. Questioning. Leaning back to get some space from me.

"Leave," he says.

"No," I say.

He steps back. Actually lifts bootheels. He has the rifle and yet he's the one weakening.

Earl is nowhere to be seen, and if I can keep George from searching the kitchen, maybe we'll make it out of here.

"Fuck. You. Thief." He takes the rifle strap off his shoulder, begins to raise it. He steps forward. The rifle barrel will touch my belly once he raises it. Not good. Before I can stop myself, I take a step back. I stumble.

"Earl is not here, you shit of a human being."

George moves closer still, too close.

I'm breathing in short shallow sips, willing Earl to stay in the kitchen. The tip of the barrel hits the zipper of my jacket.

"Maybe I should touch you? Hmm? We can play a little."

The rifle is easy to grab. It's right there and my right hand wraps around the barrel, shoving it to the left until it is clear of my body. George does not pull the trigger. He looks startled instead and then in pain. The surprise push of me on the rifle and the rifle on his arm inflames an injury he wasn't expecting to worry about. I push so hard and fast that the gun clatters to the ground. The two of us pausing to look at it down there and then up at each other.

He moves first. The blurry-pink of his fist comes at my face. His knuckles to my cheek. I sail back. Butt-to-floor reality zooming in. My back hits the diner's front door. My jaw shuts, molars fit to molars, front teeth rattling against each other, threatening to chip.

George leans in, grabs my jacket, twists his hand into leather, and swings back. Flat slaps my other cheek, unlocking my teeth and zigzagging them against each other. I feel the soft cotton of his shirt on my palm. Daddy used to wear white cotton T-shirts; they smelled like detergent.

Then something incredible happens. A little Christmas miracle. A noise. Sharp. Familiar. George looks genuinely surprised. Mouth pops open. Eyes bulge, and I turn away, afraid his eyeballs are going to fall out of his head. Then he collapses at my feet. A George paperweight to keep me from fluttering away in the breeze. He gives this little disjointed gesture, a mocking seizure move and then he begins to scream. He shrieks like a

SIXTEEN

I was bleeding when my mother found me. Ray was dead and I was leaking. The slice I opened up below my navel gushed as if it had been waiting for me to open it up all my life. Tumor. Baby. Whatever. Cut it out with a kitchen knife. It was crazy. And by *it* I mean *I* was. I know that now, but digging into my abdomen seemed like an option, as many things do, after weeks of doing harm. Ray's broken heart. My beastly one. No sleep. No food. Alcohol. Cocaine. Then some more cocaine.

That day, the 911 day, her nails were done in an appropriately dark pink, her hair was up, pulled back off her face in a soft bun. Then there was me, struggling to flush the toilet, thinking, *No one has to know*. No one has to know what we tried to do. Don't look, Mama. I'm sorry,

Mama. I was wearing black jeans around my calves. A turtleneck with a hole just above the cuff where I'd tried to dig an escape tunnel for my fidgety thumb. My black hair was toilet-water wet.

She made me dial 911. Press numbers red. She said, "I have to check on Ray." She was back pretty quickly, maybe Ray was already gone at that point, and snatched the cordless away as the ringing was answered.

"My daughter's hurt. She's lost a lot of blood. Her brother is . . . he's worse."

My mother made me throw up again. Shoved her fingers down my throat and then pressed a towel to my belly while she waited for the paramedics to arrive. When they did arrive, she told them what was going on, how long I'd been bleeding. She said, "My daughter is an addict. Like her father. I don't know what she's on." I lay still, half glazed under her hand, looking up at smooth chin, nose, and perfectly curled eyelashes, recognizing myself for the first time in her. Her cheekbones mine. Her lips mine. I didn't know she knew I was using. I thought I hid it well.

I came to again in the ambulance. One EMT and my mother. The EMT was working hard. My mother sat statue tall. Her hands folded over her knees. She looked all grown-up. Like I had finally pushed her into adulthood. Calm and smooth and cold to contrast with the dark, almost black smudge of blood I'd left over her breast right where her heart was supposed to be.

At the hospital they lifted me out. Rolled me down fluorescent-lighted hallways; I watched my mother follow and stop at the front desk. She's explaining my mess. She's still with me. I'm not alone. I focused on her heart stain until she disappeared from view.

Blood. Turns out it holds us together. Inside and out. Whether we want it to or not.

And now I'm staring at George. Someone even more successfully gutted than I. He is twitch-faced and fading. Insides oozing closer to my feet.

Earl and I are statues. Freeze-framed. Earl remains in the kitchen doorway, and I can feel the diner's front door on my back. George lies between us, a border neither of us wants to cross, and he is the only one bothering to move and he's jerking around, his brain firing out commands that make sense only to one limb at a time. If I could slice into his brain, I'd find the scene being played out over and over like something at the cinema. Me, a china doll. Dark hair without a drop of blood left in my face, skin turning to crisp porcelain that the slightest ill will could shatter. I turn my attention to Earl. His face is shifting, an arched eyebrow, twisted-lip anger. The gunshot still rings in our ears. An alive thing.

Earl opens his mouth to speak, and I wait for the hot lava to spill out.

"I didn't know I was going to do that," he says. Earl tries to drop the gun, but it's hooked into his hand like a sixth finger. He has to shake his whole arm before it thumps to the floor.

"It's good, Earl. He would have hurt you."

And George begins to scream.

A hurt-animal sound at first, but it changes, becomes thicker and darker as if he is trying to breathe but the inhale won't come. He huffs air out and wheezes it back into his lungs, a little stream. I see his belly expand and retract under his clothes, his torso swelling. It's grotesque—the blown-up dome of his body one second and then all of it caving in, making a hole of him. His mouth puckers, and for a moment he controls his breath, and in spite of the gore, I wonder if he will live. Then he is choking. The back of his head lifts off the floor and his eyes squinch shut before opening wide to match his sudden howl of a mouth. A black something, thick as tar, rises up from his throat. His teeth drown in the darkness and his screams are muffled. Then it floods out of his mouth. It pours onto his cheeks and a steam rises off him. The black liquid hits the floor and bubbles over. It mingles with George's blood, sizzling and becoming less viscous as it finds direction and flows away from me toward the kitchen doorway. Toward Earl.

Earl is too calm. He doesn't see what I see. It's not real. But then the dark blob disconnects from George, gaining a snakelike beginning and end, and Earl drops to his knees and puts out his hands.

"No! Move, Earl. Move!" But he stays exactly where

he is as the black slithers toward him, a body now more than a liquid.

I step forward, moving up next to George. I don't know what I'm planning to do, but there is sick in my throat when he lets out a low, weak whine. More a release of trapped air than an expression of emotion. His arm jerks forward, his hand shoots out toward me, but I'm too worried about Earl to avoid whatever I've got coming.

But then, nothing. George is dead, and his curled hand thumps its knuckles against my boot and lies still.

The black substance has reached Earl and Earl lets it coil up, closing his palms around it.

"It's okay, Emma," he says.

"What is it?"

"I don't know. The good parts and the bad parts?"

Earl is rolling the substance into a tight ball.

"Is it hurting you?" I ask.

He shakes his head no and opens his palms to show me a shiny, perfect ball. He moves his hands again, pinching and poking until he's given it a body and two shiny black wings. It glistens in his open palms. Earl leans in and whispers something to it and then holds his arms above his head and lets go. The object flutters and rises, catches a breeze, and floats over my head and out the diner door.

Time passes. We do not speak, we do not move. I've chewed the inside of my lip raw, my whole mouth tastes of a self-inflicted wound. Blood sweet. Salt hot. Reassuring.

The shock begins to ooze away. My body is bruised down to the bone, but nothing has gone as deep as George's gunshot wound. He's the one bleeding a thick, syrupy red.

"What the fuck was that?" I ask.

"We don't have to worry about him anymore," Earl says to me. "We can just take care of each other."

I smooth the hair off my face only to find that my palm slides a little too smoothly over my forehead. It's red, sticky. My clothes have bits of George on them. I look at George's body and see that his belly is caved in, head then neck then ribs then just the layers of his clothes cradled by jutting pelvic bones.

The world's beginning to bend, floor moving away from my feet. Quickly I sit down, head between knees. I will not pass out.

Earl sits next to me so both of us are facing George. I examine the way the blood pools into the cracks of my knuckles and the calloused skin on the heels of my hands. How would it taste?

I look long and hard at George.

"What do we do?" I say to myself.

"I love you, Emma," Earl says.

"You don't know me, Earl."

The sick comes up and I run for the door. Out of the diner, past the Jeep to kneel in the clean white snow. I expect it to be more of that black, and am relieved when it is just bile and my last few bites of food. I dig my hands in until my fingers claw pavement and scoop up snow to clean my hands, my face, the front of my jacket. I scrub my fingers red and raw. The knees of my jeans are soaked through with melted snow. Against my belly scar the snow burns deeper.

I walk on unsteady feet back into the diner.

There's a ridiculous host of items spread out around George's sprawled body. A box of bandages, medicated judging from the yellow pad on one that Earl's abandoned. A fully unrolled Ace bandage. Two rolls of paper towels, both unopened, but the plastic wrappings for three others are near a mountain of sopping red paper Earl has been using. The floor under and around George has taken on a red tint deeper and darker where the blood has pooled in the cracks. The stench is horrible, worse than blood and sweat. It's an inside smell. Private, kept safe until now. Intestines. Hurt-brown-goo bits and blood mix.

"Earl, please stop," I whisper as I move closer. I can't tell if Earl can't hear me or if he's just ignoring me. "I said stop!"

"We always clean up our own messes," he says, like he's been taught to say it by his mom along with please and thank you.

"Leave it," I say.

"We don't have to leave anything anymore!"

"What did you say?"

A new odor emanates from George's body. An intolerable and entirely human stench that even stubborn-faced Earl can't help but wiggle his nose at.

It's all about breathing: Inhale. Exhale. A body must take life in, letting it back out in equal measure. George is done with all that. Done with making. Done with destroying. Are the two always comparable, I wonder. George and I have something in common, though. I see that now. Both of us baking up dark tumors of sourness and hate. *The good parts and the bad parts.* There was no good in George, and if there was, it was Earl. And what does that mean for me?

There was never a baby in me. My body had never made anything good.

The nurses were whispering when I came to in the hospital bed post-surgery, post-everything.

"She thought she was pregnant. Poor girl thought that horrible lump was a baby. Can you imagine?"

Ray and I felt good. We had made a decision. We would take as much in as our bodies would allow and then we'd drift into death before any doctor could cut me open and prove that our baby wasn't a baby. And having that plan, a real and immediate suicide pact, was so much more powerful than any fumbling along we'd done in our lives up until that moment. It carried us through. I was so high. So close to blacking out when I decided to show Ray what I'd made for him. I wanted him to have a look at our baby before he died. See how much we loved each other. It doesn't make sense; I know that now. But then, it did. I'd taken so much from him and this was what I could give back so I wrapped my fingers around the X-Acto knife Ray used for his art projects, lifted my shirt, and pushed in. It didn't hurt at all. Not at first. The drugs made me numb and it was like watching someone else slice a piece of pie. My skin splitting neatly open. I lifted the knife away and pushed it into the round of my belly again before swiping backward so I'd have a neat slice of cake I could easily plate, but then the blood started to run out. Thick as oil. The cut began to sting, and when the pain caught me, it was so strong that I screamed, my eyes opening wide, my body propelling me toward the bathroom.

That action. That slicing open is what saved me. Without the pain I would have gone under and stayed under like Ray, though even without the pain, my body might have fought it more than Ray's body did—they said later he'd been dead a long time before my mother heard me screaming—because he'd prepped himself for the day. His body was hollowed out from sorrow and days of not eating and so it soaked up everything we gave it and greedily kept it all down. The drugs did their work and he overdosed. Gone while I was still dreaming up next steps.

Now I've got a new decision in my mind, and a warm spot in my chest to negate all the cold empty just below

SEVENTEEN

Emma!" Earl's excitement is clear. "We don't have to leave." He turns away from the diner window, his hand spread out like a fan over his scar.

"Don't talk crazy." The peace I felt moments before is gone.

"George is dead. It belongs to me. We can be *us* here." He sweeps the air around him into a one-armed hug, as if to gather up the land, the bodies, the diner, and me.

"Earl, we have to get out of here. I don't want to stay."

"We'll bring the supplies in from the Jeep. Clean up all this." He waves George away with his hand, pushing him out of the little world he only just gathered up for us. "In the summer, the ground is soft. We can grow food." He's gleeful, childish in a way that's frightening.

"You don't mean this," I say. My voice is weak. I sound distant even to myself, like an old tape recording, all garbled, rip-shredded out of the plastic case and scattered along the side of the highway.

Earl moves toward me, curls in, wraps his arms around my waist, presses the top of his head to the underside of my breasts. His request reminds me of some other time, some other person, and I shove him off. His hands unclasp at the small of my back, pull free of each other with a sucking noise.

"What's wrong?" Earl asks, as if my behavior is truly incomprehensible.

"There are dead bodies here, Earl. More than one!"

The puzzled look remains on his face.

"Look, Earl, if we stay here, your body is going to start to change. Not this year or next, but you will hit puberty and you won't be happy with what that brings. If I can get you out of here, I can get you to a doctor. They can get you testosterone or whatever."

"But it doesn't have to be a hidden place. We can bring people here. People like us who need a place."

And for a moment, I see it. A quiet place up on a hill. The diner full in the morning. Tents erected on the parking lot. A shelter. A home. It scares me how clearly I can see it.

"If it's ours, it isn't a trap. We could come and go."

"It's a dead place, Earl. We'd be snowed in all winter. There's evil here. I felt it as soon as I arrived."

"That was George! We can change it now. What did your daddy tell you? You have to want the evil. Well, we don't want it! We won't let it in."

"We are not staying, Earl. We can try to be a family, but we can't do it here."

"Please, Emma. Please."

"You'll like the real world. They can help you there," I say, and gesture to his face.

"Can they fix my scars?" he asks. I do not answer, but he takes my silence as confirmation of his truth. "I'm a made-up thing, Emma. They can't fix me."

"I'm not saying you need to be fixed."

"We're staying."

"Earl!" I shout, and he jumps. "You don't get it. I'm the evil thing! I don't have to want it or let it in. It's me. I ruin everything." I think of Ray after I had Coach Matt chased out of town. How we folded into each other even more and the real world faded away. There was just Ray and Emma and our ideas became powerful, credible—the stories we told each other were the only stories. And then Ray was gone. Story over.

I pull an old can of lighter fluid off the shelf, thinking it will get his attention. I open it and point it at the countertop. Let go. Squeeze. Let go. The tin clanks in and then out in a rush to empty then fill its own shape. I turn and squirt it in a wet S on the floor before I look at Earl.

Hand to face, mouth open slightly, eyes wide enough to show the full-moon round of his irises. I spread the stream of lighter fluid wider, letting it arc across the room.

"Don't!"

"We're leaving. You and me. Us. If I have to burn the last bits of it down to get you out of here, I will. We have to start fresh. It's our only chance."

I open a new can and toss the old one into the empty circle of floor I just came from. I dump at least half directly on George. It fizzes in his wounds. There is a book of matches in my pocket. I pull it out and light one. I drop it on George's chest and the flames snake across his surface, flowing like little rivers. For a moment the liquid is the only thing that burns and it is a controlled burn but then the smell of hot flesh mushrooms up and hits me in the face. One of the little rivers of fire snakes down George's side and onto the floor of the diner. Panic rises in my chest.

"You're ruining everything," Earl says, sounding sorry for me. Like I've lost it, like I'm the one ready for the straitjacket. He takes a step toward me and then sideways as if to step past me. He's taking his sweater off and I can tell he's going to try to put the fire out. Somehow use his sweater to smother something already set in motion. I move fast, aim at his toes, let lighter fluid barely hit. He drops the sweater and the flames rush forward as if they know it's there. It catches quickly and Earl backs toward the door.

The fumes themselves are strong, burning my throat and pushing up into my brain. They trickle down throat to chest to belly, pulsing now behind my scar. My body is flammable from the inside out. “Leave the diner,” I say, and watch his face rebuild as he decides what to do.

“I can’t.”

“I’ll take you with me. We’ll stick together. I’ll make this right. I promise.”

I’m still working my way toward the door, and as I back out, Earl follows. We make our way out into the snow. Earl, looking antsy and uncomfortable, moves back behind the gas pumps. Will they blow? The fire will never get that big, still I should move the Jeep. I’ll save Veronica if I can, but it will take too long to hook the winch up right now.

“Stay right here. Don’t move,” I say, and hop in the Jeep, driving it up to the entrance to the dark road that brought me here.

I jog back to Earl’s side, my body slowed by the snow and aching with this small effort. Earl is watching the diner. His concentration so intense that when I reach out and touch his arm he startles.

“It’s hurting,” he says.

“What’s hurting?”

“The building. The land. Can’t you hear it?”

I listen and hear only the crack and growing grumble of flames. I listen harder to the flames as they screech and crack and rattle. If I flip the noise, I hear what Earl must hear. The building screaming as the flames chew at it, taking their time. A structure whining and whistling, begging to be put out of its misery.

I take the book of matches out of my pocket and Earl whimpers. I shut my eyes. I pray. Not to God. Never to that fucker. No. I imagine the trees, our feet climbing the sap-sticky branches. Climbing above fire and bodies out into a new life. I'm doing the right thing. I open my eyes, use another match to light the whole matchbook and toss it in through the diner door. I move back. One step, two steps, three, four, until I'm beyond the old gas pumps. Earl moves so he can stand in front of me. Lighter fluid burns my nostrils so I bury my face in the top of his wild hair, and he smells warm and good and in this moment I know I don't deserve him. He killed his father to save me. His home is burning because I'm scared of staying.

This time the whimper comes from me and my sinuses burn as if I might start crying. I say: "I'll get you somewhere safe, Earl. I promise. I'm so sorry."

The flames thread their way through the maze of lighter fluid I've laid down. A flash of heat pushes up at the window.

It's time to move back. I've done what I've done and there is no changing it. I put both my hands on Earl's shoulders. His collarbone is thin under my fingertips, his shoulder blades as sharp and thin as a wishbone. He's begun to tremble. His shaking is erratic. I can feel the tension in him. The struggle to hold still, and despite the seeming frailty of his bones under my hands, he resists for a second before letting me pull him back. My hands stay on his shoulders. The crows begin to take flight. One by one they rise into the sky and head to the woods.

I hear a sound like corn popping, wood bursting open, and Earl moves suddenly, out from under my hands and past Veronica and the pumps.

"Earl!"

My hands are still curled to the shape of his shoulders and the cold air that moves over my palms burns in his absence. He's got it in his head to put the fire out again. I watch him begin to pick up snow by the handfuls and hurl it at the flames. It's pathetic, a useless gesture that is so sad I don't know what to do.

I move forward until I am by Earl's side. The building is already giving off a heat so fierce it is hard to stand this close.

"It's too late. You've got to let it all go," I say as quietly and as calmly as the burning building will allow.

"You don't understand."

"I do. I'm so sorry, but this is it."

"I can't leave." Earl straightens his spine to stand at his full height.

"Yes, you can," I say. "Those tanks could blow. We have to get out of here."

Flames join the smoke coming out of the diner doorway. The red and orange and black rises up, funneled away from us. The wind shifts. I cough and the slight inhale that follows the cough fills my lungs with smoke.

I only have to move back a few feet to find clear air. There is snow falling once again in little harmless flutters that melt as soon as they hit me. Earl is still in the smoke. It curls around him, swirls about his legs like the tail of a cat.

The diner is burning quickly, ferociously, as if it has only just found its purpose. It's eating itself. The smoke is getting thicker, blacker, and I have to cover my mouth with my jacket sleeve. The building begins to glow blue. A flame at the center, at its hottest point, burns blue and that heat is inside the building, charring the insides while the silver outside holds as steady as an oven door. I shift my line of vision back to Earl as the smoke threatens to envelop him, my eyes scratchy with soot. "Earl!" He turns, hears me. There's a crack, a loud series of pops that spiderweb the large window before sucking the pieces inward. Earl stumbles forward; the building is sucking him in.

"Earl!" My throat fills up with the stench and heat of the burning building. These hills are hungry for a few more hearts. "Earl!" This time I get a mouthful of clean air and my voice comes out strong. Please let him survive this. Please don't let me kill him too.

My eyes water and shut, and by the time I open them back up, he's there. My Earl. I can see him again. I can see all the different parts that make him up, but he is too close to the building. I know he can feel the heat through his shirtsleeves, the heat on the good half of his face.

I move through the space between us and grab his arm.

"Earl, we have to go." My muscles are tight with begging. My nonexistent insides knot up, my back folds itself origami style, just like that morning when I finally lost it. I know there's something I should say or could say to fix all this, but I can't find the words.

"I'm home. I'm already here."

"I want to be your home," I say, and the desire is so real and true and felt that I have to raise one hand to my heart and push the other into my scarred stomach to keep all the feeling inside.

"Really?" he says with so much awe and hope that I want to laugh, but then he screams. It's more pain than surprise. The sleeve of his thermal long johns is on fire. He raises it out to the side, looking at it as it arches up with orange. I bat at his burning arm with my naked palms. I feel no pain. And then we are ripping off his layers, leaving the flames behind us on the pavement, and moving farther from the heat, but it follows us. Dogged. I let Earl go.

I squeeze my eyes shut, try to hack up what's already worked its way into my system, and kneel down. My burned hands slide gratefully into the snow. As far as I can tell, Earl has moved in closer to the heart of the fire. In an effort to save his treasures or leave me behind, he's going to burn. Burn what's left of his good skin and heart in my fire, my fault.

The heat's too intense, but I want it. I want it to feel good. I want to know how it feels to be pushed up against something so hot that your skin gains muscle and willpower and curls away from the source, but I'm too weak. I have to back away a little. I've turned myself around, and I can't tell which way is in, which way is out.

The heat curves up my body before the building inhales, sucks up all the air around it, and then goes up in a fierce glare of red and smoke. I reach out again for anything to ground me. For a minute, I've got something that brushes against my fingers like cloth, like Earl's flannel shirt, and my body hiccups a little awkward sob. I grab on hard but whatever it is comes off in my hand moist and soft with heat. I drop it. I fall to my knees. Smoke rises. I'll get beneath it. I'll crawl in. Something hits my arm and then my thigh. A sharp, numbing burn like my body is being sterilized. Held over the flame until I'm hot and thin as a needle, a knife blade.

I'm bleeding. Bits of building, fire, and brick splinters rush out to meet me, gashing new wounds in my cheek, my palms. The first explosion from the tanks opens me up, reminds me that my life's thick with blood.

I've got a splinter in my upper arm that's as thick and wide as one of those fat black pencils they give you to use when you're first learning to write. I pull it out, and the wound burbles. The tanks are bound to blow and with them Veronica, and here I'll be, crawling between them, singed thin. Maybe I'm dead. Something catches me across the face, whizzing by in its hurry to get out of the center of the heat. Something else bites into the outside of my thigh and seems to want to stay there, comforted to have found a stopping point. Between the coughing, vocal cords twisting, and the tiny explosions, I catch a glimpse of Earl. I see myself at that age. Emma with her hair accidentally cut too short and fuzzing out all over her head, all dirty and lanky. Breasts not yet a threat. I want to save her, but then she raises her eyes and the scar is heating up, peeling her face away in blisters that I can tell will never heal and underneath somewhere is Earl with all his murderous mistakes and longings.

There's a boom, like a construction ball hitting a skyscraper, and the entire structure caves inward sucking the smoke in for a Kodak-clear moment. I lie belly to parking lot. There's no snow here, only hot asphalt. The heat has lessened, the air is thinning. Pine trees ahead. The pain comes as I put my hands to the pavement to crawl out. The burns coming alive in a way that makes me cry out and drop to my elbows. I army crawl away from the fire, barreling forward on soft-sore elbows. There's snow under me and stray gravel bits. I'm near the Jeep. A few gulps and I'll be ready to climb inside.

The Jeep's engine is still running and too close to the building. I need to move it farther out. I turn back to look at the burning. It's lighting up the sky and climbing the trees that stand tall all around the gas station. They're growing flimsy with fire. A matchbook hillside.

Earl.

Earl is not behind me. I rise up on my knees and peer into the smoke but see nothing. My hands are red, the palms bubbled up with blisters stiffened with pain. I stand, keep my palms raised in front of me and dive back into the smoke.

At first, I see and hear nothing. It is like the time Frank took us to the ocean. He was still wooing my mother. He drove a red convertible 1982 Chrysler LeBaron. He thought it was the coolest thing, but I knew my dad would have hated it. Like Frank, it imitated cool without understanding that being hip was meant to look effortless. Its faux leather interior with its plastic dash and its hefty top that took forever to go down. Still, I sat next to Ray in the back, and while we did not speak, we moved in close enough to share headphones. An all-day drive and when we finally hit the Atlantic the sun was setting and a storm was coming but we'd spent so much time getting there that Frank insisted on the beach, top down, waiting for all the stars to arrive.

Ray and I were restless. We leaped from that car, ran out into the near dark. The waves crashed tall and loud and because our parents were happy and distracted they did not notice me showing off for Ray as I ran into the surf. The water hit so full and cold that shock kept me from understanding what I felt was pain. Instead of fighting to find the surface, I relaxed and felt whole, until my body started awake and fought. Found the sand and pulled myself to the beach. Coughing up the water that had already swept into my lungs so eager to have me hold it.

It is like that now but with heat. The fire I walk into hurts so much and in every spot that it doesn't hurt at all. I give up on being able to see and shut my eyes. The flames wrap around me, big black bird wings that lead me to Earl. In the darkness, I find him and my body stops hurting. I pull him in, our bodies against each other, and I feel that peacefulness I felt in the ocean. All of it roaring around me as my body confuses its own strength with that of nature's. Out of the flames. I cradle Earl against my chest.

In my arms, he is a dark thing. His clothes spark and sizzle. His face dark with soot. He does not move or speak or open his eyes but I feel his heartbeat in him. It is slowed and slumbering in his chest but still there, still blessedly wicked.

Outside the Jeep I sink to my knees in snow. I press the melt of it to his hair and face. The blisters on my palms are continuing to form and dipping them into the snow brings no relief. I won't be able to hold the steering wheel like this and they will stiffen as they try to heal.

First, I lift the loose pile of Earl into the passenger seat. Second, I reach into the back and grab two of Earl's shirts and wrap them around my hands. The cotton will have to be peeled off later—I can already feel it sticking to my skin—but right now I just have to get us away from this place. That is all that matters. The Jeep door pulls open easily but loudly, echo creaking in my head. I pull myself up and in. I pull the door shut and curl my hands to the steering wheel, letting myself scream as I do it.

The rearview mirror is filled up with a glow-mask gray.

I lean forward, a quick flash of the old blue Maverick again. My mother driving me to school on a snowy morning. Not worried for once. She's laughing like the snow doesn't mean anything but hot chocolate with marshmallows. She smells like cedar and coffee.

I'm not sure I'm going in the right direction. My only consolation is that the road is tilting down at a fairly consistent angle. Sloping into ground that barely reaches past the headlights.

I'll drive straight to a hospital and tell the nurses, the doctors, that the Black Hills are burning. I'll tell anyone who will listen that the little boy with me needs help. That I set him on fire, and if they want to save him, they need to get him far, far away from me.

EPILOGUE

I've had disaster dreams for nine nights straight. Meteor crash. Tidal wave. Tornado. Campy dreams as well. New York eaten by army ants. Alien invaders. The atom bomb. Jail busts complete with nail files. And blizzard after blizzard after blizzard. I'm averaging three a night. Penance for surviving my handmade disasters.

It's dusk. The very end of it anyway, leaving me with enough light to find the path into the campground.

The road into the campground isn't impressive. It's dug deep with family-motor-home grooves. Everything around me is flat with shadows. Far off I see the threatening tilt and dip I'd recognize from *National Geographic.* I was expecting surrealism, Salvador Dalí, or at least Georgia O'Keeffe. Instead, there is a trailer park. No snow. No trees. Only small patches of cedar chips where I can pitch my tent.

I'm tired, dream-anxious. I'll set up camp, go to sleep. Dream dive. It's been strange since I hurt Earl. The dreams are horrible. I wake up sobbing, heaving like I'm trying to cough up a hairball. I want to cough it up, dislodge Earl from my lungs so I can feel free. Instead, I wake up feeling lost, but I still want them, the dreams. I crave them.

The snow has stopped coming. It's still thick on the ground up in the hills, but here, here it is just a dusting at its worst. The wind, however, is picking up speed, beating at my old-fashioned heavy green army tent. Threatening to pole snap. I should explore. Investigate what I came so far to find, but I'm tired.

The campground is surprisingly full and it takes me longer than I'd like to set up camp. The burns on my hands were largely second-degree but my palms are still wrapped in gauze and the pain is still there.

With a grimace, I push my last tent stake in and catch a curtain falling back into place at the RV closest. Someone watching me. It doesn't matter. There's nothing to see. I ease carefully into the tent. My tent blocks the wind that's pushing canvas in to touch my cheeks as I undress, arrange blankets. I curl into a fetal position. Pull up blanket layers. I try not to picture the Earl I left at the hospital. A small, all-alone boy in a too-big hospital room. His scarred face red against white sheets. His arms bandaged. Machines and tubes and pulleys meant to help him breathe and pee and hold still. They wouldn't let me see him.

In the night, however, I'd find my way to his room. They put a cop outside it—outside mine too—but the guys who came on duty at midnight felt bad for us, and they'd let me shuffle in and sit with him, rest my bandaged hands on his chest and hope somewhere in his bruised-up brain he felt the weight of me.

I picture Earl now not as I saw him last but as I wish he was. No machines, no mask. Just Earl sleeping. His small body under blankets. His eyelids resting soft and grateful. Earl. I'm sorry. I shut my eyes. Wind ripples the tent canvas.

I'm moving up out of dark. Swimming for air in my fishbowl. Kids laughing. Something clanking. A water pump? Morning dishes. Didn't sleep well. But no disasters. I open my eyes to stained canvas. There's a lump under my back. The lump shivers under the hollow spaces between my body and dirt. It squirms when I shift, moves down past my tailbone.

I crawl outside in my T-shirt and underwear to loosen a tent stake and peer underneath. A lizard darts out to stand at my bare toes blinking rapidly, shyly aware of my height. He ducks his shiny black head toward ground so I won't see so much of his half-circle smile, but the gleam of the red stripe down his back in the sunshine gives away his pride. He's as big as my foot. When I bend down to stretch a finger along his slick-oil-surface skin, he darts under the RV parked next door. I hop up on the picnic table bench to clear his path. He gives me a hiss, a tongue-drag-tail hiss as he swishes in the dirt. It's a soft hisssss, barely a threat. It starts the word going in my head again. "Hysterectomy." I remember now, last night, alone and only half asleep in the tent with the wind pushing at me, I practiced saying it slow. Hyssssssterectomy. Slower so that the *y* changes into an *i*. Hisssssssssterectomy. I like the way it slides out from between my front teeth; it's spit-slippery and sly. I drag it out at the end until it vibrates my lips. Hissssssssssterectomeeee. It sounds like the balloon-size leak that brought all of the gushy clumps out of me in the first place. Bodily fluids all mixed up until they can't even recognize their own potential. Hisssssssssssssterectomeeeeeeeeee. A word like that will upset my RV-owning neighbors.

It's morning. From atop the picnic table, I can catch a look at the landscape that juts out in crevices and pillars like shadow puppets against the faint pink skyline. My skin has begun to itch again.

I can hardly wait to change into my jeans and boots and head into the Badlands. I'll need to wear my sweater today. The wind whips up sand and cold and makes exposed skin pucker. Standing tall on the bench, my socks stuck to the wood by splinters and ancient-family-barbecue leftovers, I listen. The wind sounds different here. Different than it did in the hills. It's full of voices carried in from the surrounding highways and towns.

The curtain on the RV to my right keeps opening and shutting. Someone's peering at me. The same person from last night I'd guess. I can't really blame them. I'm standing here half naked, tent stake in hand. My legs are obscene with bruises and scrapes and goose bumps. It's impossible to shave around the traumas and so all the long black hairs stand out on end. I hop off the bench, bend down, and try to stick the stake back in the hole only the hole has already swallowed itself up. I stand up and push the heel of my foot against the stake until it slides a little farther in.

I duck into the tent to shake out my jeans. They've stiffened overnight. I check the pockets and give them one final shake to make sure there are no lizards living in the wrinkles. I bought a fisherman's sweater in the town a half hour away from the park. The sweater was five dollars. There are coffee stains on the front. Some sloppy fisherman resting his cup on his gut or, more likely, a yuppie unable to drive and sip at the same time. In either case, the sweater's warm and sloppy on my frame. With a white undershirt, it blocks the wind enough to make life outside comfortable. My hair is cleaner and softer than it has been in months, easy to braid.

I've been in hotel rooms these last nights. I took hot shower after hot shower. Scrubbed my hair with flower-woman scents.

I lean out to get my boots. I left them outside to keep from dragging in quite so much sand.

I have very little food. Some bread, apples, a granola bar, and half a pack of Life Savers. I settle in at the picnic table, which is carved deep with hearts and arrows and curse words. I run my finger along *Steve and Allison*. I have a brief flash, the couple bent over, red pocketknife digging out a picnic-table memory. Such a silly thing. I'll do the same later. Dig *Earl and Emma* into wood.

At night, I smell smoke, as if the diner and surrounding woods are still burning. When I'm sleeping, the Black Hills are not so far off and neither is the hospital that sits in their shadow with Earl in a bed, wrapped up tighter in his body than ever, the kind officer telling me that first long night: "The external burns are minor. It's the smoke inhalation that they are worried about now. They don't know when or if your daughter will wake up."

"Son. He's a boy."

"Okay. Your son."

And just like that he was my son. Mine. I felt a mix of joy and terror then that I couldn't reconcile. I did not correct the officer. Instead, in the coming days, I got quieter. Listened. Watched. It wasn't like my last hospital stay. They were kind, gentle. They all thought Earl was mine.

I finish tying up my boots and climb back into the tent one more time so that I can roll up the blankets and grab my leather jacket. I saw a phone at the entrance to the campground. I'll call, tell my mother I'm alive. I'm strong. I have a handful of quarters, dimes, nickels, but mostly pennies that I transfer to another pocket. The rest I hold in my bandaged palm and count as I walk. Nearly four dollars. I could call collect but the idea of leaving that bill behind, that reminder seems wrong. It would also give her that extra moment in which to say no, to turn me away before she's heard my voice.

The pay phone is carved up almost as badly as the picnic table. *Michael loves Nadine. Jessica and Rachel were here.* I pick up the receiver. It's ice-cream sticky, good in case my palms start to sweat. I'll still have some traction. I drop in change and listen to it clatter through, a nickel falls in the dust between my feet. There's a pause before the phone begins to ring. The old pale blue rotary phone sitting on the end table in the living room, each ring rattling the metal handle on the drawer. My mother finishing up breakfast dishes. Shaking the soap off her hands, drying them as she walks to the phone. Flats squeaking on linoleum and then shuffling onto living room carpet. It rings four times, five.

"Hello."

I can hear the distance between us static and pulsing. I don't know what to say first. I should hang up before the phone line clicks dead. I press my finger deep into my other ear, but I can still hear the kids playing freeze tag behind me in the campground.

"It's Emma. Are you there?" I press my finger deeper still until all I can hear is my blood pumping. The silence doesn't become any clearer.

"Yes. I'm here." Her voice is dotted with miles.

"I wanted to call." I hold the receiver closer to my mouth. My chin presses to the black plastic; my bottom lip grooves into the tiny holes.

"Where are you?" She's brittle and anger flimsy. I could scatter her with one slam of the phone. I hadn't expected to have any power.

"Far away. And, well, things haven't been so good for me." I dig my thumbnail into the groove of *Tess and Amelia Friends4Ever.*

"Yeah, well, things have been hard for all of us." She spits it out quick either because she hasn't meant to say it just yet or because she's anxious to point out my mistake. "I'm sorry, Emma. I didn't mean that. Are you all right?"

There's a faint noise, a click. I squeeze the receiver harder, press it against my ear.

"Are you there?"

"I'm here," she says. I hear her suck air, hold it, and then continue.

"I've done a lot of things I can't take back," I say.

"Oh Emma. We all have."

"I want to get healthy," I blurt out.

"You mean you want the radiation?" I can tell she is trying hard not to sound excited. She doesn't want to scare me away.

"I mean I want to stop using. Drugs. And people. I want to get the cancer out of my body. I want these burns to heal."

"What burns?"

"Nothing. I mean it doesn't matter. I just want to heal."

"I want that for you too."

"Mom," I say testing out the word.

"Yes," she says. The test a success. She accepts this word from me, likes it even. I can hear relief in her voice.

"I wanted it to be a baby," I say suddenly. "I thought I could be a better parent than you and Daddy. Like I would know all the mistakes not to make. Now I'm glad it wasn't real. I would have fucked it up. There is no way I could raise a child."

"Emma," she says as if my name is the only thing she is certain of.

"I'm too selfish."

"Everyone is selfish at eighteen. You're supposed to be selfish. I was selfish! I didn't want a baby. I got pregnant and I knew I had to have you, but I'd hit my belly with my fist every morning."

"Jesus. That's a horrible thing to say."

"Wait. Let me finish. Then, after you were born, I loved you so much that I knew what I felt for your father and what he felt for me had never been enough. Not really. Not for a lifetime. And I knew that my world could be bigger with you in it. All those little things I used to worry about became insignificant. There was just you and me. That's what mattered."

"I don't know what all that means for me now."

"Trying to save your father from himself almost killed me. Choosing to be your mom though . . . well, that saved me, Emma. You are my family. Always will be no matter what you do." She pauses before asking, "Are you okay?"

"I am okay."

"Are you safe?"

I think about that word "safe" for a while and all that a mother might mean by asking it and then answer: "I am safe, Mom. I'm okay."

"I love you, Emma."

She wants me to say it back, but I can't so I say, "I'll call you in a few days and . . ." The phone goes dead. *Thank you for choosing us as your long-distance carrier.* I keep the receiver pressed tight to my ear, dead dial tone cuts in. I grip it tightly until it begins to beep loud and harsh. I hang up with my free hand, hold it down but keep the phone to my ear for another minute.

I walk back to my tent, focus on the sifting of the sand away from my boots. I need to get inside the tent. Sit for a minute where no one can see me. "Family." The word is thumping around in my belly, pushing against absent organs, begging to burst open my ugly scar. "Love." That's another good one I'll never understand. The word begins and ends with a sound so soft, so gentle yet it congeals on my tongue. It doesn't hiss or howl or swoosh. It only sits there, mouth rotting.

Nine days ago, I drove up to an emergency hospital entrance. Slammed brakes into a skid, dragged myself out, bleeding, aching, crying, shrapnel-pincushion Emma. I hobbled through sliding doors, latched on to a nurse, a doctor, some woman in mint-green scrubs. I told them Earl was still in the Jeep.

"There's a fire in the hills. My little boy got hurt. I couldn't get him out fast enough. Please, save him." I was still really scared. Suddenly sure I could have done more for Earl if I'd only tried harder, tried sooner. I said, "He's hurt bad. Please hurry," and then I passed out. I crawl inside the dirty-green-dome tent, lie flat on my back, and cover my eyes with my hands, press my thumbs into eyelids. Behind them is a smiling Ray I don't want to concentrate on, but I zoom in again, pull up his face. I can feel the rolls of the blanket under my butt, my jacket and shirt pulled up so that a strip of skin touches the wool itch. I should fix it, but I relax my arms instead, leave my palms over my eyes to keep in the dark. Ray's face has changed to Earl's. One soft cheek and one scarred cheek.

I'm crying. I feel tears working through the grooves around my eyes before they slide down over the edge and pool in my ears, ocean-salt sounds.

My curled body aches hiccups. I breathe deep. I feel soggy and red. My eyes are burning. I'll just rest, picture black. Just for a minute and then I'll go exploring. I'll wash my face at the pump and then I'll go.

Earl. Burned-faced, angry Earl. He's sitting at the corner of the tent, his hospital bed under him, hunched up, drawing on his dangerously pale outstretched leg. He's holding a shiny silver pen, like a blade, that moves in tight, slow strokes. The pen must hurt him so I whisper, "I'm right here." He looks at me and smiles, trying to make me smile. Eyes, violet, near purple. A fuzzy-peach velvet. I want to touch his pupils, the pits of his eyes. I reach out, inches from that purple-blue when I notice his scabs. They're a deep ashy black, thick like charcoal and beginning to slide down his face. The scabs are pulling the wrinkled skin down, leaving behind a smooth, natural, fleshy pink. Like a fancy theater-house curtain falling down to the stage floor. Down from cheekbone to cheek until it all hangs soft off Earl's jawline, dangerously loose. I turn my outstretched hand palm up to catch the moldable pink mass of ash and scar, but it changes again. Turns to liquid, a silver-gray mercury that drops onto my palm, a metallic puddle that slides even and wormlike over the wrinkles of my skin. Earl's rising, getting up out of his hospital bed to leave the tent that's grown to circus size. He stops when his head reaches the canvas top and looks at my liquid palm.

"I'll be there soon," I whisper to Earl, and the liquid begins to move, glide quicksilver to my wrist along the inside of my arm up the curve of my armpit, around and under my breasts, cold down my torso to my belly button where it pools thick, turning to a charcoal ash, warming me straight through.

Acknowledgments

This book has been in the works for a long-ass time. Earl and Emma first met in a college playwriting class, so thank you to Antioch College, and to all the fabulous professors I met while I was a student there. Thank you too to Jessica Wallis, who during that same period of time took that fateful road trip with me that landed us in the Badlands and the Black Hills. Perhaps we would have had more energy for hiking if we had eaten something other than pancakes?

While the inspiration for the book began in college, the first draft came to life at Emerson College, where I had the privilege to work with Jessica Treadway and Christopher Tilghman. Special thanks to my good friend and fellow grad student Eric Mulder, who believed in the book way back when.

Thank you to the members of the Yellow Springs Writers' Group and the Quarry Hollow Writers' Retreat. Thank you to the Antioch Writers' Workshop and Tin House Summer Workshop. Special thanks to the Ohio Arts Council, which not only offered me a grant but also introduced me to the Fine Arts Work Center in Provincetown, Massachusetts. Thanks to Tom Jenks and *Narrative Magazine*. Thank you to Pam Houston for introducing me to Writing by Writers and the talented Christian Kiefer. Mary Carroll Moore, I am indebted to you for your wise editorial comments and for sharing your own inspiring work with me. I am forever grateful to Debbie Phipps Pretzel Chips for telling me it was time to leap.

Thanks to Antioch College, the Miami Valley School, and the Moses Brown School. These institutions believed in me when I'm pretty sure I knew nothing at all about writing, teaching, or leadership. I owe a great deal to my students, who have taught me about who I want to be—in particular, Rafael Torch, whose ferocity and talent will always inspire me. You are missed. Thank you to Eli Nettles, who always calls me out when I'm being a "titty baby," and to the text string Dermit for making me take life less seriously. To Michelle Martello, Annie Branning, and Katrina Kittle for never giving up on this book. To my parents, my little brother, the Wallis family, and the town of Yellow Springs. You raised me to believe that the life of an artist was well worth pursuing.

I am grateful to Dawn Tripp, who helped me find my fierce and supportive agent, Kimberly Witherspoon, and equally thankful to Kim, who connected me with my editor at MCD, Daphne Durham, who, with the help of Lydia Zoells, has shaped this book into something I am really proud of.

And, most of all, gratitude and love to my spouse, Daniel Meiser. My home will always be with you. And to my daughters—Violet Hays (ten) and The Wilde Beast (eight), who are already the strongest, funniest, smartest young women I know. Be unstoppable.